THE HARE AT DARK HOLLOW

THE HARE AT DARK HOLLOW

JOYCE STRANGER

Illustrated by Charles Pickard

TARGET

First published in Great Britain by J. M. Dent & Sons Ltd, 1973

First published in this edition by Tandem Publishing Ltd, 1975

ISBN 0 426 11009 9

This book is fiction. All the people and places in it are imaginary.

Target Books are published by Tandem Publishing Ltd, 14 Gloucester Road, London SW7. A Howard & Wyndham Company.

Printed in Great Britain by The Anchor Press Ltd, and bound by Wm Brendon & Son Ltd, both of Tiptree, Essex

Specially for Joanna

My thanks are due to Mr Timmis, assistant curator of Chester Zoo, who very kindly allowed me to see original papers and books belonging to the Zoo, and who sorted out the relevant chapters for me before I arrived. Also to Dr Maurice Burton who helped with information.

Contents

I

Dark Hollow

There had been hares on the land at Dark Hollow for longer than men could remember. Usually only one could be seen at a time, but there were often several running crazy under the March moons.

Kee lived there now. Her home included the Five Acre field, which was starvation poor, a sorry ground of thistle and nettle, groundsel, ragwort and dock growing among spiky grass. It continued to the farthermost edge of Hawkoak wood. It was bounded on the west by the cornfield belonging to Dark Hollow Farm, and on the east by the dense shrubby copse in the centre of which was the Dark Hollow itself, a secret, hidden, sloping depression in the bottom of which was a deep pool. Willows arched above the water. A kingfisher nested in a hole in the bank and was sometimes glimpsed, a jewelflash in the gloaming, but for the most part the Dark Hollow was a hidden corner known to no one except Crook Weller, the old poacher who liked to lurk there and watch the hare as she moved about her ground.

Sometimes Kee caught the stink of Crook Weller, and heard him as he pounded over the Five Acre field, on his own bewildering business.

There were other noises. Far away, the sound of car engines and, intermittently, the sudden swelling rattle of a train, and its cry in the night, a hooter blare. Kee was a brown hare, richly coloured chestnut, and soft grey and white, with long spoon ears and upturned whitebacked tail. She was part of the wild, and so had her ancestors been, and her whole world was there, a limited world of a few hundred acres of familiar ground.

She did not know that change was in the air. One evening, men came to the Five Acre and paced its boundaries, eyed the wood and looked in the heart of Dark Hollow. She could not understand the deep voices. There were two men. One, she had seen before—a thickset, redfaced man with a harsh voice that often rose in anger. Matt Grant, who farmed Dark Hollow Farm, was short tempered and impatient. The other man was slender and small, pale-faced and soft-voiced, and he moved delicately over the muddy ground, as if afraid of dirtying his beautifully-shod feet.

The men talked together for a long time, while Kee hid in the grass, almost under their feet, and dared not stir, lest they stopped and grabbed her, or had some strange means of catching her. She was so still that neither man noticed her. She could smell the cows on Matt Grant's clothes, and there was a smell that was odd about the other man, a smell that made her sneeze suddenly, softly, mouth closed. It was the smell of soap, of course, unknown to Kee.

The men heard the sneeze and looked about them, but still saw nothing. At last they left, and when Kee was sure that the field was hers again, she sat up and cleaned first one ear and then the other, sliding each between her two front paws. She bounded across the field, leaping high in the tall grass to look about her. Crook

Weller, passing along the line of the wall, noted her and went his way. He had other ploys in mind at that moment and there were trout in the pool in Dark Hollow.

Summer turned to autumn and autumn to winter again. Kee had known the late April snow the year before, but this time the snow lay for days, and life was uncomfortable. She dug under the white carpet for moss and lichen and pine needles, and managed to survive.

The new year, the year of change, was also the year of the Great Wind, and Kee's life took a new path, as did that of all the creatures near Dark Hollow.

For a little while longer everything continued as before. There was no foreknowledge of impending doom. No glimpse of the astonishing happenings that were to come to Dark Hollow. No inkling that this was the end to all that they knew, for the creatures who lived there.

Time was running out for Dark Hollow. Yet none of this was known to Kee.

Her life went on as before.

2

Kee's Family

Kee had many enemies, and she knew them all by sight
and by smell. Scent was more potent than name, for Kee
had no language.

There was Red Ruin the fox, with his gaping mouth
and hot tongue and eager eyes, who made frequent havoc
in rabbit warren and duck pond and hen coop, having
turned rogue in his prime. Though he hunted never so
carefully, hiding his scent on the wind, Kee's long ears
caught the pad, pad, pad of his paws, and the rustle of
his coming in the grass, and she was gone, leaving only a
delectable smell of her own on the ground that made the
fox slaver and lick his chops.

There was tabby Tibb, from Crook Weller's home on
the far side of the hill. Crook Weller, the farm folk said,
was a no-good nobody, a poacher, a thief and a rogue.
He was a gaunt old man with sly eyes and clever hands,
who kept to himself and heeded nobody. Some years
before he had bought an old bus and removed its wheels,
and he lived inside its rusting body in squalid content
with Tibb. Tibb came stalking in the moonlight, eyes
glowing with the lust to kill.

There was Weh the weasel, slip-sliding on stealthy feet,
able to sneak in and out of a burrow and take what he

would; there was Starra the stoat, little as the weasel and as great an enemy.

These were the creatures that prowled on the ground.

There was Hoo the owl, floating through the dark, his wail awakening terror, so that the hares crouched and the tiny leverets froze close against the earth.

There was Harc the falcon, crying his harsh call, and Craw the crow, danger to anything small that lingered in reach of his dagger beak. There was Kigh the kestrel, and the merlin, Mille. There was Mah the magpie, with his spearlike beak.

These were the creatures that struck from the air.

Last of all, and more dangerous than all of them, there was Crook the human, with his old gun and his lurcher cur, Dago. Kee had heard the gun speak. The word it spoke was death, and she saw one of the Jack Hares roll and somersault, twitch and lie still, and be lifted by his hind legs and swung from a vast, careless hand. She did not yet know that there were worse perils than the rusty gun, or the slavering jaws of the cur that spent most of its life tied on a rope beneath the old bus.

Each day of the year brought her new knowledge. She knew the chilly feel of the starry dark, and she knew the glowing light that hung in the midnight sky. She knew the warmth of the midsummer sun, hot on her fur as she drowsed on her form, ears always alert, eyes watchful.

The days of winter had been hard to learn, for food was scarce and buried deep, and deer and pony, hare and rabbit, had to paw at the ground and dig before finding even thin nourishment.

With spring came Dag, a buck hare, older than Kee by twelve full moons. He stayed with Kee for a while and then left her. She continued to roam. Her ways always crossed under the stone wall, through a gap that had been there for many hare generations, and where she, in her turn, sometimes crouched and watched, being anxious not to run headlong into danger.

In the days that followed her sojourn with Dag, she wandered along, or basked in the sun, never relaxing her guard. She no longer wanted to play, or to leap lithely over the grass, or, as she sometimes did, to bound across the ditch and soar over the little wall that bordered the lane. Not even moonlight tempted her to whirl and spin in delight. She watched the rabbit games from the shadows, and crept back to her hollow of dry leaves and grasses, and her look-out post under the hedge on the hill. Here she could see all around her, and in that lay her safety.

When the stirrings inside her could not be denied, she looked for a sanctuary in which her leverets might be born. She needed space, for none could lie near another. Each must lie alone, but first, they would all be born together, and then she must carry each one to a safer place. There was danger in their first hours on earth, for Weh or Starra might scent the birth smell and come on silent feet and rob her.

The Five Acre field was large and patched by furze and bramble. Tall spiky grasses grew in solid clumps and ragwort lifted its leafy head, as yet showing no promise of the yellow flowers that were death to sheep and cattle. She bounded slowly, stopping often to look about her lest danger come stalking.

In the middle of the field was an oak that had withstood the winds for more than three hundred years. Its roots, buried in sandy soil, were clenched and knotted, straining from the earth, trapping thick leafy mats that enticed many small creatures. It scattered broken twigs liberally around it, so that many small birds rustled beneath its branches, hunting for nesting material.

Here, deep underground, was a vast chamber in which the old badger lay, sleepy with age. His mate lay elsewhere, guarding her young. As Kee came by, searching for a safe birthplace, old Bracky poked his battle-scarred nose from the set entrance. The wind told him of beetles and mice, but did not bring news of Kee, for the breeze blew from him to her. As soon as he moved away, she bounded across the Five Acre field, her breath harsh in her throat, her small heart pounding.

Nothing followed her. She rested, but her time was short and her need was urgent. She slipped through the hole in the wall and found safety in long grass at the edge of the wood. There, in the darkness, her babies were born. She felt deep satisfaction as she washed each one with a careful tongue, nuzzling it close.

There was little time to spare. As soon as the younglings were dry, Kee took the first in gentle jaws and slipped through the gap. She laid it in a grass clump beneath a whin bush and leaped away, mazing her trail back to the birthplace. Before the moon had dived behind the horizon, Kee had all four leverets safe, all in the Five Acre field, but each one far from the others.

Much of Kee's time was taken with visiting each leveret in turn. The babies lay quiet knowing, by instinct, that safety lay in perfect stillness. Crouched in long grass, their world was bounded by light and dark, by sunshine and starshine, by rain, and by the thin wind that keened constantly, talking in the trees and whining in the wire that carried electricity over the field to the faraway Dark Hollow Farm. When the wind blew strong from the west, the leverets heard the cows at Dark Hollow, but never, in all their lives, did they discover what strange creatures made the plaintive sounds. They did not travel in that direction, although the farm lay on the edge of the Five Acre.

Their early days were a sleeping and a waking, to find Kee beside them, mothering them, cleaning them, giving them brief protection. She dodged all round the field before coming to any of them, masking her trail so that no beast could follow her. She slept alone, in her high place, and her ears warned her of danger long before danger came.

One day a strange man arrived and brought with him an astonishing four-legged creature, with a high bray that called disconsolately when the man had gone. Kee did not know that this was a baby donkey, feeding like her on the grass, and that it offered no harm, except that its small hooves might possibly crush the babies beneath them. She watched it anxiously as it stood forlorn and lonely, having just been taken from its mother and wanting her warmth. Kee moved her own babies that night and hid them in the wood.

The little hares had been born with open eyes and fully furred. They lay snug, each in its own haven, and watched the strangeness about them. There was the inexplicable movement of cloud above them, and the equally strange way in which, sometimes, warmth lapped them in comfort, and the sky was still, and at others they were soaked and chilled and the sky was torn by rushing

18

grey masses. Before two weeks were ended Kee could tell her leverets apart.

There was Rik, a little buck, bold and over inquisitive, but luckily endowed with a brain that was to serve him well all his life and get him out of frequent trouble. There was Lyn who, when she was grown, would look very like her mother but, unlike Kee, was timid and gentle: there was Mali, bossy and bumptious, butting at Kee in blustering welcome, another little doe: and lastly there was Tip, the little one, who would never heed a warning, and who was far too adventurous and had not Rik's power of thought.

There came the day of Rik's first adventure. He knew, by now, about light and dark, and he was beginning to know smells. There were so many, from the scent of the crushed earth, bruised beyond the wall by the hooves of the little donkey: of thyme, pungent-sweet, that Kee sometimes broke when she browsed, and which scented her naked pads. There was the sharp tang of the wood after rain, and the nose-stinging smell of the patch of wild garlic leaves beyond the ditch. There was once a terrifying choking reek that made Rik shudder as Red Ruin ran past and dug at the ground with a lazy paw, trying to find young rabbits deep in a burrow. But the fox was full fed and digging in mischief, and wild garlic masked the hare smell.

Red Ruin loped away, and Rik noted the smell and Kee hissed a sharp outdrawn breath when she caught the tell-tale of the fox's passing and, for one heart-searing moment, thought Rik had gone. But he had merely drawn deeper into the grass clump. He met her with uplifted face and she basked warm and content as she fed him. He stored the fox knowledge deep in his mind, not yet knowing why, but aware that he must.

Kee could never tell the leverets of danger. She could show them and warn them, and push them with her nose. They had to learn daily, and they had to learn fast. Much knowledge was born in them, bred there by perilous centuries, and they knew well that the wind was saying, with every whine and whistle and whimper, 'Learn well, little one. Learn well, or you will never live to see many moons pass across the sky.' There was so much to learn, and never time to relax, or be heedless.

Rik learned the fastest. To him the world was all excitement, a place of constant movement, of swaying grasses and shivering leaves, of flying shadows and scudding clouds. It was a world of astounding shapes, that ran, or scurried, or flew, or prowled. It was a world built for giants, where a baby hare was so small and defenceless, so soft, so overwhelmed that it could only lie close against the ground, and huddle and shake and stare and hope that nothing would come near.

Soon the leverets were exploring, learning to run and walk and bound, each watching Kee as she leapt towards them, envious of her long legs and the great jumps that she made. Rik made his first bound and tangled his legs with a thorny bramble twig that thrust itself towards him, grabbing him. He tore away terrified by its tenacity; the searing thorns left a mark that hurt for days, which he licked, time and again, to soothe away the pain.

On their fifth night on earth Weh the weasel caught the scent of little Lyn, and slid along the ditch towards her, his eyes eager and his lips slavering. Lyn was mesmerized by the night, for when she had first seen

light there had been a full yellow globe above her that hurt her eyes when she looked up, and now, mysteriously, the globe had vanished and there was a tiny golden crescent that shed only a soft glow around it, and feathered a trail of cloud mist with shining brilliance. The previous nights had been moonless. The clouds slipped away and spumed into glinting foam and were gone, and in that moment Lyn caught Weh's ghastly terror-inspiring tang, and leaped sideways, as Kee had taught her, and crept beneath a rock that offered shelter. Weh fished beneath it with his paw and she caught a whiff of his breath. The panting that he made accelerated every heartbeat. Tabby Tibb, passing, saw the weasel and pounced. It was Weh's turn to run, pellmell, headlong. He was young, and not yet strong enough to fight a cat. They vanished and Lyn stayed still, quivering. Kee, visiting, knew the weasel had been by from the scent on the ground. She licked her small daughter and comforted her.

It was windy. The leverets had not yet heard a high wind, and watched in astonishment as all around them giant trunks swayed and creaked. Branches groaned as a half-gale raced madly among them, and the hares sheltered, afraid of the noise. The invisible tormentor stroked fur the wrong way and, where the earth nearby was bare, blew grains of sand into Lyn's eyes, making them sore. She retreated into the darkness and comparative peace beneath the rock, and there not even Kee could follow her. Kee went to find Mali, who was sniffing the boisterous air.

Mali had been watching a beetle crawl beneath her paws. It was the first time she had seen anything alive that was smaller than herself, and her eyes followed the blueblack body as it scurried busily across a bare patch of earth, its clawed feet making a whispering noise. Mali focussed her ears, intrigued. She touched the beetle with an exploratory nose, but disliked the feel of the horny body.

Later that same evening Rik ventured farther. He made a little angry noise, like a small snake hissing, a sharp-blown breath, no more, as a tangle of straw blew across his face. He pawed it away, frenzied, and it fell to one side and he tapped it. It was harmless, but for one moment he was sure that it threatened his life, and his pulses raced. Then he settled again, and seeing his mother coming, he bounded towards her.

There was a faint hoot downwind. Hoo was hunting. Kee heard him coming and froze against the ground. Rik mimicked her at once, so that all Hoo saw was two rounded dark stones, motionless against the grass. He did not look farther. He needed prey that moved and ran. Beyond was a mouse, its thin tail twitching, a moving telltale.

Rik saw the swift shape that was Hoo slide down the wind on wide wings, and swoop. He heard the panic mousecry as one of the mice found a sudden end under Hoo's clutching talons. He felt the fear that lay in the air stemming from the cry, and the horror of the dark shadow that swept above him. He had learned a new lesson. That hunting shadow would never catch him in the open. When Hoo's white wings shivered the darkness, Rik would always be gone.

Kee was beside him, and for a few rare moments he snuggled warmly against her, sucking life. It was lonely for a small leveret in the big spaces by himself, but he did not feel a lack. Briefly, Kee nosed him, and licked his soft fur, revelling in her son. She knew that he had seen the mouse die, and would mark it well. She herself, when only three moons had slipped across the night skies of her life, had raced from the swinging darkness that fled across the ground in front of the owl, when the moon itself was a glowing gold orb, a full moon, a hunter's moon, offering scant safety to the little creatures that sped from its treacherous light.

3

Dangers

The days that followed were growing and learning days.
They were also days on which change came to Dark
Hollow, bringing new perils. The farm was sold and the
farmhouse stood empty. The cattle left for new homes.
Only the sheep remained, for they belonged to Pennyplacer and not to Dark Hollow. Crook Weller, knowing
others would harvest the cornfield, set three snares.

Safety for the leverets lay in hiding. Deep in the waving
grass, little brown balls of fur lay as still as the nearby
stones. There was never a quiver or twitch to catch the
eye of the windhover as he hung on the air : never a
twist or tremor to catch the attention of the great crow :
never a flicker of an eyelid to make the sparrowhawk
look again.

There were so many dangers. Safety, almost always,
lay in feigning death. Lie still, small one, said the hare
with her body and her urgent nose, as she left each baby
after suckling it. Hide, and never move, lest the fleeting
fox whose smell lies rank on the grass should see a paw
twitch. Learn the musky throat-tightening stink of Red
Ruin, the killer. Lie close, and hope that he does not
catch the faintest scent that will tell him of your presence.

Hide, lest the plunging hawk take you to his fledglings :
watch the land and watch the sky and see how his wings

blot the blue: see how his shadow races towards you, faster than rainclouds masking the sun. Lie close in the palpitating dark when Hoo the owl swoops swift. Listen for his calls, for his wings are noiseless and he comes mothlike out of the night. Hide, little one, lie closer than darkness: never mind a thumping heart or shaking fear that bids you run. Lie, stiller than death itself, under the waving grasses, and no creature will see, or scent, or hear. Lie still.

Safety lies in stillness, savouring the pungent night. Learn the night noises. Learn, and never stop. Is it a mouse that is hiding, or is it Weh the weasel waiting to pounce, or Starra the stoat on velvet pads, creeping, or lying, sinuously curled, his bright bilberry-button eyes watching from behind the thick bole of the oak tree: or perhaps it is tabby Tibb, sitting watching so innocently, his tail curled round his plump body, his red tongue lick-licking over his narrow lips, his green eyes bright in the shuddering darkness. Learn them all, and remember. Smell of fox and cat and weasel. Smell of bird. Smell of danger. Fearsmell. Terror smell. Noise in the dark, pad, padding. Learn. Learn. Learn.

Safety lies in listening ears, able to detect the finger-light footfall of an ant on a blade of grass: ears able to identify the sigh of a frightened mouse, pressed tight into a narrow crack in the oak's thick bark: or the sudden whirr and start of a jumping grasshopper, or the shout of a nearby cricket, over and over, on and on: or the angry call of a bird, yelling into a quiet sky. Heed them all, small creatures, and lie closer than ever when they shout fox! fox! fox!

Safety lies in sensitive paws which can feel the shake of

the ground. It may be the donkey running in the field, or it may be that cool naked pads have recognized the thumps as Crook Weller, the giant with cruel fingers, pounds his massive booted feet on the turf and swings his death-dealing gun to his shoulder.

Kee conveyed her thoughts as she fed the leverets. They were not language thoughts, but feeling thoughts, so that she crouched, stiller than they, when the owl winged downwind. She imbued them with her fear as the fox loped softly past. They watched her, seeing her constantly twitching nose, her ears, moving backwards and forwards like sensitive antennae to collect the sounds and sort them, and hear danger loudly above all other noises. Relax, it is only the startled deer. Be wary and still and hold on to every breath as the fox flees past, a running rabbit stampeding in front of him. Tighten every muscle, for the thud, thud, thud is man, cruellest enemy of all.

Rik lay close and watched the world from his nest. He could see the sky plainly. The grass hid everything that was level with his nose. He could hear all kinds of sounds. The constant plaint of the unknown creature that sang in the wires was an ever-present mysterious background, a reminder of things unseen. Sometimes it hummed softly, and at others it twanged harshly, and at times it was masked by the raging invisible wind that could make life a total misery. There was most danger when the wind blew strong, for then Red Ruin could approach unheard, and Weh could slide without betraying noise, and Starra could pounce, and the noisy creatures of the air hid all of their comings.

Rik explored when the nights were quiet and he could

hear plainly. He never roved far from his grass nest. If a tremor shook the ground, or a strange cry tortured the air, he was at once crouched in hiding, never moving hair or whisker. Even his ears lay flat on his head, close against his body. The moonslip fattened, and flung its brilliance among the trees, so that the shadows were dark pools in which fear lurked. Kee had learned to use the shadows to hide her coming, but the moving leaves, reflected on the ground, worried Rik, so that a thousand times a night he stopped in dread and hid, not knowing that the swaying shadows were never a threat.

Before he started he tested the breeze—only the scent of flowers and mosses and the tang of wild garlic, only the freshness of grass after the rain shower that had ended an hour before. He bounded high, experimenting, and landed on a thistle that bit his small pads. He leaped to cover, puzzled by the plant that had the power to hurt and, as he had with the bramble tear, he licked away at the soreness, trying to wash it off. Next time he avoided the thistle patch as well as the tugging bramble sprawl.

The grass was thick and the wind blew through it. Somewhere, not so far away for Kee, but an endless distance for Rik, was the cornfield. It lay across the donkey field, through the gap in the stone wall and beyond the ditch. It lay beyond a thick thorny hedge. The inch-high green was nectar, an enormous temptation to Kee, who spent some of her nights there, browsing and growing fat. The taste of it was sweet on her tongue when she washed her babies, and they learned the smell from her.

One night Kee, in her comings and goings, discovered a corner tainted by man. His stink lay strong and, as she left the field to return to the leverets, she heard a cry from the grass. Curious, she loped across and discovered a rabbit swinging high, his neck newly broken in a snare's noose. She hurried away, skirting the corner, eyes wide with terror at the new and unguessable menace that lurked in the cornfield.

Beyond the cornfield was the sheepfield. The woolly greybacks were familiar and roused no fear in Kee. She knew the lambs, heady with excitement, standing with mother all day, and then suddenly, before the sun went down, congregating together to play for an hour while the ewes rested.

At the end of their playtime the ewes called to them, harsh mother bleat answered by high pitched baas, and as the flock sorted itself out again into mother and baby, the air was loud with their cries. Kee knew what made them, but the hiding leverets could only listen, knowing that the same noise came each afternoon just before five, but never knowing why.

The sheep feared little except the running fox and the old sheepdog Mick from Pennyplacer Farm. They were a threat to Kee and the leverets too. Mick had gone bad, and lived on the fells. There was a burning pain in his head that could never be appeased, for he had a growth there. He hated men, and he hated the sheep that once he had tended, and the killing lust was on his tongue, and there were guns waiting for him. Fear of guns had taught him cunning.

One night Rik crouched in total terror as Mick ran among the sheep, leaping at throat and rump, never quite drawing blood. The sheep milled and dodged and panic-bleated in horrid clamour that brought the shepherd running, another sheepdog at his heels. Mick tore away through the hedge, leaving a gap through which two lambs escaped next day and, darting over the ditch, he clambered over the wall and landed in the Five Acre field. He crossed it as the shepherd sent a charge of shot speeding after him, and reached the far wall that bordered the wood.

There was a gap beneath where a broken drainpipe lay open to the sky. A moment, and Mick was through. He was hungry and angry, and he caught the scent of leveret, and was on top of Mali before she had time to cry. When Kee came to feed her, there was only a trace of fur and blood. Only three leverets were left. None of the others knew what had happened to their sister, but Kee knew. Mick's scent lay strong, and she would know it again, but there was nothing she could do. She went to nurse her other younglings, and was forlorn, coming back twice to smell at the nestplace where Mali had lain, as if hoping she could conjure her back to life again. The leverets were only three weeks old.

Rik, that night, lay and watched the glowing globe in the sky pull wisps of mist across its face and hide itself. Then came the strangeness that he hated, for with it, always, came a chilling wind as water dropped from the clouds and soaked his fur, and drummed on the ground.

By morning the rain had ceased and the clouds were stretched thin across a remote exhausted blue and the sun woke a steamy gauze that hid the grass. Rik nosed it, a little fearfully, wondering at the wreaths of cottonfroth nothings that parted to reveal bramble bush and tree-trunk, and then returned, and lay damply about him, making bright droplets on his thick coat. Kee came out of the dimness, looming above him, startling him for a moment before he turned to her for comfort. She nosed him and he knew that she was unafraid, and he relaxed.

The strengthening sun banished the mist and warmed small chilled creatures and dried damp fur. The sun was hotter than it had ever been in the leverets' small lives, and they basked in its comfort. The wind had forgotten the wood and gone elsewhere. Everything was unusually quiet. Not a leaf shivered and, with the stillness, all the birds relaxed too. Rik lifted his face to the sky and the sun filled his eyes and was a searing pain so that he had to look away and cover his face with his paws to shut out the brilliance. It was yet another memory to store away. He could look endlessly at the night-time light without harm.

Sunshine was a new world. A blackbird dropped to land on a twig not a foot above Rik's head, and the leveret stared at the glossy body and burnished bill, at the small bright considering eyes that looked down at him, and he listened in astonishment to the sounds that came from its quivering throat. It seemed an immense bird, bigger than him. He had never seen a bird close before and he was surprised when it opened its wings and flew off and he realized that it was one of the creatures that often soared across his horizon.

By noon a small wind was teasing the grasses. Rik lay absorbing noise and light and pattern, watching shadows steal mysteriously down on him and vanish, feeling the chill as a cloud sped over the sun throwing darkness on the ground. He crouched close, sheltering, as the wind began to frisk the trees. Seven more days and nights passed by, each the same as the day before. Then came change. Rik did not know that that was the last day his mother would come to him. He was a month old and grown and already nibbling the grasses. He had learned more than he knew.

When Kee did not arrive, Rik began to wander in search of tastier food. He browsed throughtfully in the last hours of light, and suddenly, came a warning—clarion call from blackbird, thrush and starling; echo from robin and wren: shout of chiffchaff and warbler and yell of the angry pheasant. The little hare was too far from cover and crouched flat, a brown bulge against the leafy ground. Then came the angry rattling whicker of the magpie and the jay's terrible scream. All the sounds meant the same. Run, those who must run. Fly, those who can fly. Hide, those who freeze when death comes walking.

Does danger come racing on four red foxlegs? Is it death in the ditch with the sliding weasel? Or is it Tibb that comes pat-patting, delicate soft paws hiding armoured claws?

Does danger loom above on owl-wings, on hawk-wings, or eagle-wings? Or on the wings of the dainty merlin, or of the glorious falcon? Watch, said the birdnotes, all you creatures that hide in the grass. Hide and tremble. Hide. Or run.

There was a scar across the sun. There was a shadow racing swiftly over the grass. There was a death threat cleaving through the air, and Rik saw it come towards him and knew that it came for him. He leaped sideways. farther and faster than ever before, and sideways again, and there was a sharp thump as the hawk hit the ground, finding nothing. Rik did not wait for the bird to recover

its wits, but leaped into the bramble tangle, oblivious of clawing thorns. He made his way through the dense tunnel, and crouched in the green dimness, his heart racing.

The hawk soared to the top of a blighted tree, watched for movement, and waited. Nothing moved. Only the wind stirred the grass.

Rik hid in the bramble thicket for the rest of that day. Beyond him, once, he felt the earth tremble as Crook Weller thumped across the ground, intent on his own affairs. He caught the rank smell of Dago, the lop-eared black cur. The hawk flew away and Rik dozed and woke and dozed again, until the sky darkened and the moon slid over the horizon, to mark the end of another day safely passed.

Rik came out to nibble the grass stems under the moon and thought that he was wise. He did not know that he was very young, and had everything to learn. Kee had left him. He was now on his own, and every creature that prowled or flew knew that.

The darkness brooded. The owl cried, and the wind stroked soft fur with silken fingers and the only creature moving in the wood was a small brown hare, his ears alert for every sound, and his eyes bright with suspicion.

4

The Storm

By the time that two moons had grown fat, and died, and begun to shimmer again, Rik and his brother and sister were beginning to explore. Rik learned the ways that led to his feeding places, following the beaten track, pounded out by many paws over many generations.

There was the trail from the wood, through the rustling dry ditch where piled leaves crackled underfoot: it led up the edge of the ditch, where a young hare could sit and test the wind, and watch the flying shadows. Is it owl that casts darkness over the ground as he watches and waits, or the shadow of a bush flung sideways by the moon? Each flicker of movement made Rik crouch, and freeze against the ground, his ears lying flat on his head, his breath barely moving his furry body. His eyes, set at the sides of his head, saw plainly to right and left, and even behind him, but looking in front was more difficult.

All was still, and he bounded on, through the hole in the wall and into the moonlit Five Acre field, where the donkey browsed. Rik and Tip and Lyn knew the donkey now, and knew the beast offered no harm, though, when it lifted its head and yelled at the night, they crouched in sudden fright. Only the scolding pheasant made a worse noise.

On the first night of their ninth week on earth, the three leverets met in the field and began to play. It was a ghost-filled night, the wind a soft sigh in the trees, each leaf drop plain to hear, so that their chasing game was often interrupted. They trusted nothing, and stopped to listen to every new sound. Their eyes and their ears were their guardians : they dared not relax. Kee watched them from the shelter of the wood, but did not join them. They were old enough to look after themselves, and her task was ended. She made her way by another trail to her favourite feeding place in the cornfield. Later that night she would venture into the farm garden and feed on the new-growing parsley. She forgot the leverets.

Rik was filled with delight. The moon above him, the murmuring wind in the trees, the sighing branches, were wild excitement. He bounded high, leaping over Tip, and the two began to run in a giddy circle. Lyn was feeding, having found a patch of ground where clover grew thickly. She browsed happily, content, pausing at intervals to listen, sitting erect, her eyes searching the field. Once she stopped eating to clean her ears, running each paw caressingly over the fur, smoothing it against the skin.

When she had finished, she crouched again, and watched the field about her, sneezing once, mouth shut, a small stifled sound that caused the other two leverets to turn towards her, and then, reassured, to turn away again and continue their chase. Once Rik leaped high over Tip and caught him with his hind legs, rolling him, and Tip retaliated as soon as he had regained his breath. It was a mock battle, meaning nothing, a game between brothers, but it was preparation for the future, when Jack hare might fight Jack hare in earnest, both wanting the same doe. Speed and quickness of reaction could only be learned by practice.

There was a snuffle in the grass, a rustle, and a padding. Lyn gnashed her teeth, a sharp, angry rasping sound and, at once, the field was still, and three motionless brown lumps blended with the long grass. The snuffling came close and the young hares looked in astonishment at the spiny creature that paused, rooting in the soil, ignoring them. The hedgehog went on towards the ditch and vanished, but long minutes passed before the leverets were sure that all was safe, and began to feed.

There was a murmur of unease on the hill. The sheep were anxious. One bleated, and another, and then another. A few moments later they were racing, running, huddling, hiding among each other, jumping in panic disorder, every beast baaing loudly as Mick, the killer sheepdog from Pennyplacer, came in their midst. He chased among them for a few minutes, but the pain in his head made him slow and stupid, and he grew bored with their noise and massing bodies, and went through the hole in the wall into the Five Acre field.

The hares were still, but Mick's sensitive nose caught the scent that lay about the hole in the wall, and he followed Rik's track until he came to the feeding place. Rik knew the dog was hunting on scent and, as the animal came towards him, he exploded from the ground in a sudden movement that startled the sheepdog so that he paused, and in that second Rik was away, running for his life, long hind legs bounding, ears flat against his head.

Behind him came the padding paws and sniffing nose

and panting breath of the sheepdog. Across the Five Acre field went Rik, over tussock and whin, leaping sideways and starting off again, twisting, turning, mazing, trying to increase the distance between the hunter and his quarry.

At the end of the Five Acre field was a stream, a lazy shallow thrust of water that surged slowly over a peaty bed, ending in the deep pool in Dark Hollow. It was only four feet wide, and Rik leaped it, and set off again. The sheepdog, following, splashed noisily through the water, slowing almost to a standstill. Rik bounded on, his breath catching his throat, his heart as noisy as his bounding pads.

Overhead the owl called, *hoo, hoo,* and turned aside to take part in the chase, and his swinging shadow swooped ahead of him. The moon shone, uncaring on the three—Rik, the crazed sheepdog and the watchful owl.

Along the hard trail to the cornfield, over the ditch and over the wall he ran, with death pad-padding behind : through the new-grown corn, to shy away from the taint of man in the angle of the field, and to crouch low, panting, hidden from Hoo. The owl flew off, disappointed, and his sweeping shadow fled before him. The dog circled the field, knowing his quarry lay near, then yelped in sudden anguish as the hidden noose caught his throat and lifted him, struggling against it. In the morning the farmer from Pennyplacer found him there, and put an end to him, thankful that there would be no more sheep killing. There was no cure for a dog gone bad.

The night was almost done before Rik recovered from his run, and began to feed on the sweet corn blades. He browsed slowly, aware that he had weathered another hazard. He did not know what had happened to his tormentor.

When the birds called to the sun to welcome it over the horizon, Rik lolloped slowly along the road beside the cornfield. He was aware of sound long before he saw its cause. He had never heard a noise like it before. It approached him, rising to a crescendo roar, to a full throated bellow that was accompanied by a demon honking, louder even than that of an angered cock pheasant. The creature flew towards him, its increasing clamour deafening him. It was immense, larger than any moving thing that he had ever seen, and he leaped into the ditch and crouched until it had passed him. The children in the car saw his fleeing body and shouted:

'There's a hare!'

The words were flung by the wind, and Rik heard the shout, but it was as meaningless as the monster that had hurtled towards him, and he noted that there was yet another menace in his world. He noted too the smell that came with it, and learned to avoid roads whenever possible. He quivered at the sound of a car whenever he heard it, until he realized the monsters never left the hard roads.

It had been an eventful night that taught him more than he had learned in all the weeks before. He took the trail back, leaping the stream, crossing the Five Acre field, creeping through the hole in the wall, and into the wood.

Dawn had come, but the sky had vanished in a skirl of thick, grey-mottled cloud. The days before had been hot, and he had spent them lying in a scrape in the gound in an open covert, where the sun beat down on his fur and

he basked in drowsy warmth. Today the wind was
needling and he left his previous bed and found a cosier
hide among the whins in the long grass, sheltered from
the inquisitive fingers that poked and pried into every
cranny.

Darkness returned, bewilderingly by day, so that
birds cried uneasily. The wind strengthened. It howled
down the hill and fled among the trees, furiously blustering. Branches tossed and flung themselves skywards, the
trunks creaking and groaning. The gale came from
across the sea, the fiercest wind that ever that part of the
land had known. A branch tore from a tree near Rik,
the noise of its rending even louder than that of the car
that had passed him in the dawnlight. When the earth
had stopped shuddering Rik crept out from his form,
and sought shelter in a hollow away from the wood.

All day the wind rioted. Leaves blew across the grass,
the corn was swayed by waves that flattened it from wall-
side to the far hedge and, as it stood erect, flattened it
yet again. The elm tree in the far corner of the wood, hit
by a gust that tore across the sky, scudding the fleeing
clouds, ruptured its roots and crashed to the ground, and
every bird and beast within range of its dying cries
quivered with fear.

Kee herself had never known wind like this and
crouched in her form at the far end of the Five Acre field,
listening, while the three young hares flattened themselves against the ground, and shivered in terror.

The long day ended, but the wind left them no peace.
The earth was dry and small drifts of dust were blown
in their eyes. Rik tried to clean his with his paws, and
Lyn hid deep in shaking grass, and Tip found another

place to lie. They turned away from the wind and huddled against the ground. Darkness fell, and nightmare began.

The overburdened clouds burst, rain drummed noisily on dry soil, arrowing through the night, lashing at fur and feather until every creature was soaked. Hailstones hammered from the sky, bruising defenceless bodies. There was little shelter, no relief from discomfort, and no respite from the wind that howled in the wood, and flattened the corn. There was no peace anywhere.

Red Ruin lay deep in his earth, listening to the turmoil above him. He, at least, was dry. The hedgehog crouched under leaves, curled into a tight ball. Four squirrels left their dreys, and found harbour in rabbit burrows.

Lyn, desperate, hid under the hole in the wall, out of the rain. The wind struck the wall full force and flattened it, and Lyn did not live to see daylight come on a ravaged world. Now there were only two of Kee's leverets left.

Darkness surrounded Rik all through the endless night.

Birds, in the shrieking trees, shrieked too. Jay and blackbird, crow and magpie, dove and robin, sparrow and heron, hawk and owl, all cried in fear, and the noise that they made drowned the wind-noise. Crouched in their burrows, in quiet shelter, the rabbits listened. Mice hid under roots. Weh the weasel lurked in a foxhole, and old Bracky tucked himself deep underground and stayed out of the storm.

There had never been such a wind in living memory. Just before daybreak, it whirled to a cyclone and caught at small bushes, ripping them from the ground. It caught up twigs and leaves and branches and even bowled over

41

the sheep, and tossed the little donkey sideways to lie flat against the wall, all the breath knocked from her body. It tossed Rik, too, so that he was caught and flung against a tree. Then, as suddenly as it had come, the whirlwind died. The gusting gale paused for breath, riven clouds parted to show a spangled sky, and a watery sun shone on a world that had changed overnight, where destruction was supreme, and where yesterday's growing bushes were now lying on the ground, their roots already drying in the breeze. The rain had gone, but the sodden earth was a morass and movement was misery. Rik cleaned himself, and scratched his ear, and tried to clean again. He squeezed his long ears between his two front paws, removing the surplus rain. He shook himself, but remained uncomfortable. He gave up. He could only wait until his fur was dry.

His bruised body ached, he had damaged his paw, and he limped as he moved painfully through the wood. He huddled forlornly in a shallow dip, from which he could see all around him. The world had changed overnight. Trees, snatched from the soil, thrust tangled roots skywards. Light shone where there had been no light before. Pools of water lay in the hollows. The birds were looking for new nesting places, and the long line of the greystone wall was broken in several places.

The donkey's owner came to survey the damage, and to look at the little beast, which also limped badly. Rik watched the man examine the slender legs, and go away again, and return, some hours later, with yet another man, whose skilled hands felt over every inch of the donkey's body.

'What a night,' the man said feelingly.

42

The Vet nodded. He stood up and dusted his hands together.

'She'll be all right.' His quick eyes glanced about him, noting the damage. He saw a small brown body half-hidden by undergrowth at the edge of the wood. Rik did not even twitch an ear, and the Vet said nothing. He preferred to let wild creatures live their own lives, undisturbed by man, and hares did little harm. Perhaps a nibble at a growing crop. There had been one in his own turnips the night before. He did not know that it was Kee who had fed there leaving a telltale, for hares stripped off the turnip skins, but rabbits ate them. It had certainly been a hare who fed so choosily along the furrows.

The men went away, the donkey began to graze, and Rik drew a short sharp breath of relief, and sneezed gently to himself, warm at last after the long chill night.

He did not know that this was the last of the peaceful days, and that men would come to his quiet home, to remedy the damage made by the Great Wind. Life would never be the same again in Hawkoak Wood, or in the Five Acre field. There were changes due, and there would only be uneasy resting places for the creatures that belonged.

5

The Lurcher

The wood became an unhappy place, where men with tools worked all day and the chatter of their tongues and the shrieking, brain piercing whine of their saws drove the beasts away. Kee no longer took the trail to the farm. Rik watched the men from safe hiding, deep in Dark Hollow, and lay still until they had gone and the wood was quiet again before he went to browse in the Five Acre field. But even here there were changes. Men walked the length and breadth of it each day, and harsh voices threatened the restless air. Men with revolutionary ideas were planning new uses for the Five Acre field. The old farmhouse was knocked down, its dying a crash and clash and thunder that bewildered the birds and the beasts and drove them into cover.

Rik no longer visited the wood, but turned instead to the stream across which he had bounded, running from the dog. Here rain had fallen in such quantities that the far end of the Five Acre was flooded. A lake lay there where no lake had ever been before.

He sat and stared at it, puzzled. He skirted the water, and returned to the clover patch. The donkey was feeding close by, but they ignored each other. Neither was a threat to the other.

Rik was bewildered by the noisy saws, by the thud of

many human feet, by the changes that had come to his home place. He forgot to watch for the fleeting shadow that raced before the hawk. His first warning came from a sudden yell from the blackbird and he bounded sideways by quick instinct and again the hawk missed and hit the ground. Rik fled, uphill, and that was when Crook Weller saw him. Coming towards Hawkoak Wood to gather dead sticks for firewood, he saw the bounding hare and loosed his cur.

'Fetch her then, kill'er then,' he said, all hares being she. Witch's creature, devil beast, the hare. Crook was an old man, a simple man, who had never been to school. He had been brought up by his grandmother, who believed in spells and witchcraft, who made cough cures from herbs picked under the waning moon, and planted her garden only when the moon sat right in the sky. She had always said the hare was a thing of evil and this Crook believed, though he was not averse to putting it in the pot. Nothing like a jugged hare, thick and juicy with gravy, tender in the mouth. His eyes brightened at the thought.

Dago, let off his leash, was wild with excitement. He had caught the hare scent, and was hunting on the trail, the wind blowing in his face, the scent strong on the wind. His long legs raced over the ground.

Rik was running for his life, but this was not the first time. This time, he knew tricks and wiles and twists and turns, and he had to shift his ground, and get in front of the betraying wind. He turned on his own trail and ran back fast and leaped sideways, so that the lurcher, now hunting on scent alone, checked, puzzled, as the trail vanished. He cast about, and Crook, who had been

46

watching, tried to direct the cur, but was too far away. Dago was ill trained and ignored his master's whistle.

Rik ran through the wind-scarred wood and leaped the wall on the far side. Dago, casting again, found the new trail and raced after. Across the road and through the cornpatch fled Rik, over the ditch and over another wall, down a long lane with horror close behind, death a heart-throb away, and with panting breath, choking throat and searing pain under ribs already bruised and sore. Leap aside, and twist and turn. Jink and dance and slip away, but never fast enough to increase the lead. Never fast enough to get away, never fast enough to leave the speeding cur behind.

The birds were calling now, warning of danger running on four feet on the hard lane surface : warning of the hunting dog, sliding across the ditch, only a handbreadth from the hare. Rik heard them and sped on. There was no second chance, no future. Nothing was left to him but speed and cunning.

Run, little hare, run down the wind and outpace your enemy, called the robin, chattering from a nearby bush, as the two fled past. Run, little hare, run away.

Run away, run away, the echoes repeated and the noise of the birds increased and Crook Weller, limping hurriedly after the two animals, yelled his encouragement.

'Get 'er, Dago. Good lad. Go on then,' and Dago tried to obey, but he too was feeling the effect of running far and fast, and his legs were failing.

Crook yelled again, and waved his disreputable hat, and the dog struggled to catch up. Slowly, Rik was gaining, and the distance between dog and hare increased until they circled on their tracks and came again to a standing part of the greystone wall round the Five Acre field. Rik gathered his strength and leaped sideways, jumping as far as he knew how, and cleared six feet, to land close against the wall. There was a small gap beneath the stones and he squeezed himself inside and crouched, trying to stifle his rasping breath, lying quieter than moonbeams on downland, listening to the panting cur.

Dago came to the end of the trail. He cast again, but could not find the scent. He tried and tried again, and Crook, who had been unable to keep up and had not seen the young hare run for cover, encouraged the dog, but it was useless. Dago had lost all heart and presently, with tail tucked between his legs, he crept to his master, who cuffed him in fury and turned on his heel and walked away, while Dago followed, head and tail hanging.

It was a long time before Rik crept out. He left the wall, and zig-zagged down the gently sloping hill to the Five Acre, and here he found Tip feeding. Kee had left the wood, and kept now to the edge of the farmland. Men had come to her territory and she knew men were dangerous, beyond all reason. They could kill with a running dog: they could kill with a strangling noose: they could kill with the stick that spoke and crashed its sudden thunder and sent hares flying tumble over, tumble under, to lie still and smell of death.

Rik and Tip did not yet know all this. They played at tag and at tussle-wrestle under the moon: fed and listened and played again. They leaped over one another, boxing in fun, fighting together, to leap away, and race one another to the far end of the Five Acre and stare in puzzlement at the spreading water that had buried the best patch of feeding in the whole field.

That night they followed Kee's trail to the cornfield and found the sweet tasting blades, and fed until they were full. That night they fed too well—the farmer swore revenge.

6

Fire!

The moon grew fat and died again to a straw in the sky, barely visible, and the saws rasped and whined in the wood. Men cut logs, and gathered brushwood into piles, and removed the wall.

The undergrowth in the wood was trampled, and muddy patches grew bigger. Rains came and turned the ground into a sodden marsh. There were no longer trees to protect the ground and soak up the excess moisture. Lorries came to the far lane and dragged away the sawn-up trunks. Bustle and noise and shouting voices marred the peace. Then the sun came back and dried the muddy ground, and red dust flew where men's feet walked.

There was nowhere for the birds to nest, and they left. The squirrels also went abroad to find trees that would shelter them safely. They took up new residence in a little copse behind a new estate, and the children, as they walked to school, watched their slender beautiful bodies flying through the trees.

One of the men sent three rabbits to a quick end with shot. Rik saw it happen.

One evening a boy came to the wood to find free kindling. He picked up a stick and aimed it, and said 'Bang' at the sky, and Rik was off, his legs carrying him far and fast at such a speed that he never realized that there had been no accompanying crash and flash. The boy did not even glimpse the hare. He was not country bred, and had no eye for movement.

Rik hid in the shelter of a bush that had not been torn up by the gale, or uprooted by the men. His ears listened and his eyes watched. The boy sat comfortably with his back against a tree stump. The wood was almost clear of large trees now, and only the aftermath remained : sawdust and shavings and papery dead leaves and thin, brittle twigs.

The boy was free and on his own, away, briefly, from adults. He could do things he dared not do at home. He took a cigarette out of his pocket, and a box of matches. He struck a match, lit the cigarette, inhaled deeply and then choked. Choking was uncomfortable and, as he struggled to regain his breath, he tossed the match away. It fell into a patch of dead leaves.

A little telltale of blue smoke eddied and vanished. The boy, still choking, crushed out the cigarette beneath his heel. It had been bitter disappointment.

The boy ran home and forgot he had ever been in the wood. Behind him, the small telltale smouldered, and a blue wreath floated gently into the air. Rik's quick nose caught a strange smell and wrinkled, puzzled. Farther down the Five Acre the donkey lifted her head, uneasy, smelling something she had never smelled before, and Tip sat and sniffed the wind, not at all sure that this new smell was not a threat of some yet unknown form of killer. None of the three relaxed.

The wind had been resting but, as dusk crept over the sky, it began to wake and whisper in the grass. Small eddies gusted the leaves and stirred them, and stirred the little smouldering heap, blowing on it caressingly, until a small red glow burned in the heart of it. Then the wind fanned it softly, so that it began to breed, first on the leaves around the little heap, and then on a dry dead stick. The fire was alive, a slow trail and fast flicker, feeding on everything that stood in its way.

The infant fire grew stronger, a steady flash and crackle, a spill of flame as the wind blew a burning twig which landed in a pile of dry powdery wood, fallen from the sawblade.

The creatures in the wood were alert, sitting and sniffing, wide-eyed and anxious. A flame rose from the tossing brushwood and caught at another, larger pile, and with the flames came the wind, to send the fire rolling over the ground, through the dying undergrowth, through the few remaining trees. A dead pine flashed to brilliant blazing life. The sudden flaunt of flame that seared its tall trunk was a signal to the people of Penny-placer Farm, where someone raced to the telephone and alerted the fire brigade.

There was panic in the wood. Weh the weasel forgot his hunting and ran from the heat and the din, while behind him came his mate and four hungry youngsters. Kee was safe, but Rik and Tip bolted from the angry night, speeding towards the water, while Starra followed, his clawed feet whispering over the ground, and the hedgehog's clumsy body raced over the uneven tussocks in the big field. Hoo the owl came crying from the trees, narrowly avoiding setting his tail feathers alight.

The cock pheasant plummeted out of the ground with a rush of wings and the hen gathered her chicks and bolted them over the wall. No need to tell any small thing to hurry. Fear hung over all of them. Fear of the lights in the night, of the choking smoke tearing at every throat, of the flash and dance and flight of the fire, and the fear was compounded by the screaming terror that came clanging along the lane, bell sounding, men ready to leap down and fight the enemy that had been loosed among them. This time the men meant safety, but none of the flying beasts knew that. Only the donkey, used to man, came to them for comfort as they brought the hoses to the water, unrolled them over the field and directed the full spate of the nozzle against the leaping fire.

All the beasts had fled to the sanctuary of Dark Hollow. Here, they were far enough from the wood for safety. The grass in the field was too damp to catch fire. The bushes in Dark Hollow sheltered them from the eye-searing flames. Rik lay close under a sorrel clump, his heart racing because he could not understand what was happening.

There was noise all round him. The wind whipped through the Hollow. That, at least, was a noise that he knew and recognized. The ground throbbed, a giant throbbing louder and more earth-shaking than running hooves on the turf, a thud and thunder and constant tremor under his paws.

Above the thump of the engine came the seething swish of water from the hoses, and above the roar and crackle and sharp cracks of the flames came the steady zithing hiss of water on hot fire, soothing it to silence, to darkness, to a sodden morass of black ash.

Evening came, but still the men and the fire fought a grim battle. One fireman was burnt by a falling branch, and added to the noise was the roar of the ambulance as it approached, the din of its siren, and the screaming of the police car that came to the scene. The animals crouched even lower and trembled. There was wickedness abroad in the dusk. There were unknown evils in the wood. There were giants and roaring demons, there were trolls and panic-mad hobgoblins, there were unknowable beasts and unguessable dangers. Dangers that were worse than the swooping hawk, for the hawk betrayed himself by his shadow, and could be dodged—worse than the running dog, for the dog betrayed himself by his panting, and could be outrun—worse than the slavering fox, for the wind betrayed him often enough, and he too could be outwitted. But here were new perils, and they did not give any warning of their coming. They sprang out of the ground, as the fire had sprung. They roared towards the wood, as the car had roared. They were terrifying because they could never be understood.

At last there was no more fire. The pumps stopped, the hoses dried up, and everything was loaded again. The fire engine and the police car drove away.

There were no more trees in the Hawkoak Wood. The fire had completed the destruction wrought by the saws. There was no more green. There was no more food, and nowhere, under the star-crazed sky, was there any protection.

When all was quiet again and the sun was no more than a rumour before dawn, Rik bounded out of Dark Hollow and went cautiously to the edge of the wood.

He did not go in. The aftermath of fire was sour in his nostrils, a sharp pungent reek like nothing he had smelled before. It caught his throat, and stung his eyes, and it marred his fur, so that much later, when he tried to

groom himself, he tasted woodsmoke, bitter against his tongue. The grass in the field, too, tasted of smoke. The corn at the edge of the cornfield was blackened, and farther into the field the growing shoots were tainted. He went back to Dark Hollow and fed by the little spring, where the grass was lush and sweet.

Later that day Rik watched from the edge of the Hollow as more men came to survey the damage, shook their heads, and walked about the scarred ground, their voices rising and falling as the wind flirted among the bushes in the Hollow.

They went away. Rik lay and watched all day, and only when the moon pierced the cloud wraith did he dare to move and browse by the new lake, which was far from the wood. Here Tip was also feeding, browsing fat on sow thistles and chicory and rich green clover.

Rik was even more wary than before. He eyed the wood distrustfully, not at all sure that it would not leap into destructive life once more. Then, suddenly, he felt a betraying tremor in the ground, and stamped and rasped his teeth sharply.

When Crook Weller reached the field there was no sign of either hare. He scanned the moonlit grass, but nothing moved. He walked through the desolate wood. There was not a scrap of kindling left. No pheasant lay close in the dead undergrowth. He hunted until dawn, but his search was futile—the fire had driven all the beasts away. It did not occur to him to look for them in Dark Hollow.

He went, and the robin was left chanting his warning.

Trust nothing. Trust nothing. Trust no one.

Beware.

Rik heard, and lay close to the ground, ears flat on his back, a little brown tummock that seemed devoid of life.

The hovering hawk, hanging on the airslips, did not catch a tremor of movement from the grasses that hid the hare.

7

Changes

A month passed without incident, and Rik and his brother grew. Both were larger now, long-legged and thickening in the body. Rik's markings included more white than his brother's. His eyes were darker and his whiskers longer. The quiet month gave them time to strengthen their muscles, and to perfect their leaping, so that, when each returned to his own form, he made two immense bounds that killed all scent, and left him in safety.

Men came to look at the field and the wood, but they were not interested in the beasts, and saw nothing of them. They were not even aware of the angry birdcalls that heralded their coming. They knew nothing of the hares that watched them from Dark Hollow, and lay quiet, and only relaxed when the intruders had gone again. Rik loved the sunshine and panted with pleasure when he was alone, and sneezed to himself comfortably and silently, warmly basking in blissful solitude. If the sun was too hot he sought shade, and if the wind was intrusive, he found shelter from it behind a stump or knoll which gave him protection but did not completely block his view. He listened constantly to the birdcalls, knowing that they would warn him at once of danger.

Weh and Starra did not trouble him. There were

young rabbits in the field, and the pheasants had chicks and the ducks had young. There were many unwary that fell victim. Sometimes the questing stoat and the stealthy weasel slipped across country to the haystacks and wrought havoc among the wicked rats that bedevilled the farm cats. The rats bred too fast. Not even owl and hawk and slinking stoat could defeat them as they harassed the henruns, stole the eggs and killed the chicks. One of them, an old and vicious grandfather, killed four of Grey Cat's kits. The farmer found her lying beside the despoiled nestplace that she had made. She was sick with grief and cried for her lost young, and he lifted her and took her indoors by the fire for warmth and the comfort of human hands, and the farmwife soothed her with milk and a soft voice.

Grey Cat forgot the dead kittens, but she did not forget the comfort of the farm kitchen and from then on she was a house cat and not a farmyard cat. It was her privilege to drink the creamy milk first and her place was on the hearthrug. When work was briefly set aside and the farmwife rested, Grey Cat climbed on to the soft lap and her rumbling purr of content filled the room and drowned the angry chatter of the whirring clock.

She heard, too, the conversation of the farm folk at Pennyplacer. Had she understood and been able to pass on the news, she would have known that soon there would be turmoil all around her, for the owner of the land had auctioned the wood and the Five Acre field, and it had been bought by the men who had bought Dark Hollow Farm. The people at Pennyplacer speculated and worried and wondered, and rumours ran swifter than stoatpounce wherever there were men to indulge in guesses.

There were to be caravans on the Five Acre field, and stockcar racing at the far side of it. No, that was wrong. There were to be more donkeys and a funfair. There was to be a chip shop and a dance hall. No, there were other plans. There was to be a supermarket and a town complex was to be started that would, in time, overrun all the country around and even Pennyplacer would have to be sold.

There was to be a zoo. No, there was to be a wildlife sanctuary. No, there was to be a garage. No, there was to be a new factory, sprawling for miles, its chimneys pumping foul chemicals into the clean air. No, there was to be a prison.

No one, from day to day, knew what story would come next. Meanwhile men and machines were moving in, giant pumps were working on the flooded portion of the field, men were scoring the black earth in the wood and, as the noise rose to a crescendo and even stranger machinery was brought into the Five Acre, more of the beasts left.

Weh and Starra and their families moved to safer quarters a mile away, where man was only a brief intruder. Kee kept to the far edge of her homerun.

Old Bracky, finding the desecrated wood a horrifying place, sought out an ancient deserted sett among trees to the west of Hawkoak. Badgers had lived there once, but had been killed on the roads as they travelled in search of food. Bracky dug out the tunnels and took in fresh bedding, carrying armfuls of bracken which he cut with his teeth, still sharp enough for that. He shuffled along, entering the sett backwards, and all the time he sniffed the air for telltales and listened for sounds that would warn him of danger. Nobody came. It was quiet in the West Wood. He settled there as if he had always belonged, and his mate came too, with her cubs. Only one man knew that badgers had come back to West Wood, and that was the Vet, whose house stood at its edge. He saw the new diggings and the fresh turned earth, and was glad. Man owned too much of the world for his liking, and he hoped the West Wood would remain untouched.

Rik kept to the centre of Dark Hollow, where sunlight slanted through thick trees, and dappled on turfy slopes beside the singing stream. Here came many of the birds that survived the fire, and made new nests. Some had lost their eggs, and laid again. A mallard drake and duck found sanctuary, and the drake was watcher for all of them. His bright little eyes saw everything, and his angry hissing, a noise quite unlike the contented quack that he had used when talking to his mate, alerted all the other birds.

Rik learned to melt into nowhere at the first hiss. His splendid spoon-like ears caught the slightest sound, so that he was aware of the soft plump of a frog on the ground beside the water, of the rustle as a bird's sharp little claws moved on a dry leaf, of the angry hawing of the donkey, as they loaded her into a horsebox and drove her away. She had been part of his background for the whole of his life, and he watched, puzzled, as men urged her into the darkness of the strange contraption in the field, and drove her off. The owner of the land had sold her too, and she was going to strangers.

That night he loped slowly towards the field, where huge machines crouched blindly, awaiting the men who animated them each day. He had already learned that they only lived when men were there, and that at night they slept and he could browse in the grass, right up to their wheels, without them making one single movement towards him. He watched them carefully for a week before he dared trust them. The big bulldozer was parked each night beside his favourite patch of sow thistles, and hunger made him bold. He was ready to leap away should the sleeping beast stir, but there was a never a shudder or whisper after the men had gone.

Once his fur brushed against the cold metal and he sprang sideways, leaping farther than he had ever leaped before, sure that the Thing had reached out and touched him. His heart raced and there was a thickness in his throat. Nothing moved. Only a cloud sped across the moon, and the moon vanished in brief darkness and came out again. All was still. Not even the wind whined, for the trees had gone and there was not enough breeze to stir the grasses. Rik recovered his confidence and began to feed again, but he did not relax.

The sounds that reached him were known sounds. He sat erect, and looked about him.

The intruders might be coming his way, or they might not. Better to freeze against the ground than to run, for the moment. He crouched in the grass, his ears flat on his back, the moon highlighting his gleaming fur. There were several creatures abroad that night.

The first that approached came ponderously, not bothering to hide his coming, rustling in the grass sniffing and panting, brushing carelessly against the looming bulldozer as if aware of its impotence. It was only the hedgehog, prowling by himself.

Uzzi went on, his odd agile legs carrying him at a

great rate over the ground. He was retracing an old trail he knew well, skirting the water, hastening along the road to Pennyplacer, where, if he was lucky, the outdoor cats would have left some milk in their bowls and he could steal it. He adored milk. Sometimes he found a spilled pool near the cowshed and lapped at it, his small eyes watchful, ready to run should men appear, or one of the sharp-eared dogs, but while he drank, he savoured total bliss, for there was nothing in the whole world that Uzzi like as much as milk.

He did not know that the small girl at Pennyplacer was aware of his coming and put a bowl down especially for him and, sometimes, she was awake to watch him take it. He was sure he was thieving, coming on the saucer unseen, serenely unaware that he was welcome. He retreated afterwards to the garden and the haystacks, where he more than repaid the farmfolk for his milk by killing slugs and beetles, and young rats when he found them. If he also took a nibble along the furrows, nobody complained.

Rik watched Uzzi pass. Uzzi turned his head. He might, if he could, kill a leveret, or feed on a hare that the fox had left, but he did not kill for the sake of killing and Rik was safe. He did not know that he had only been spared on previous encounters because Uzzi was not hungry. He would be secure in future, because if Uzzi turned towards him, Rik would be off, trusting nothing.

There were more noises. Far away, the unknown, unimaginable invisible monster that was a diesel train rattled through the darkness and cried its sorrowful warning as it entered the tunnel. Overhead one of the enormous birds that glinted in the sunlight, and showed strange-coloured, glittering, winking lights at night, roared on its way across the continents. It had traced a path through that part of the sky every night since Rik was born, and its companions passed by day. He did not heed them now, though at first he had quaked in terror when the planes flew over, not knowing that they would never stoop as the hawk stooped, to hurtle out of the air and annihilate him.

The plane had hidden other sounds. When it had gone, the whisper on the ground was a thunderous shake, and Rik was caught unawares. Crook Weller was hunting. He was out for what he could find, and tonight, afraid that men from the building operations might come back and challenge him, not knowing that they had no knowledge of any beasts at all where they were working, he had left gun and dog at home, so that he would have an innocent explanation for his foray. He was unable to sleep ,and had come out for air. He had also come out to investigate the snares he had hidden in the cornfield. Crook did not yet know that the farmer at Pennyplacer had bought the cornfield at the auction and, after finding his old sheepdog in a snare, had searched in the field and removed the others he found. He did not like them, any more than had the farmer at Dark Hollow. But they had served a useful purpose in putting an end to Mick. The Vet had wanted to find out what had been wrong with Mick and had discovered the growth in the animal's brain, that explained his wild behaviour. No creature could have lived long with that.

Crook came upon Rik, lying flat against the ground, and his quick eyes saw him. Nothing escaped Crook. He had only a stick with him, and he poked it at the hare.

Rik was erect in a second, boxing at the stick that threatened to savage him. He leaped clean between Crook's legs and away, his long bounds taking him out of reach within seconds. Crook, startled by the attack, roared with laughter, entertained by the sudden viciousness and the flying body, and vowed to get the hare on another night. The animal could not last long when there was so much destruction going on around him. Soon there would be nowhere to hide.

A moment later, it was doubtful whether Rik would survive long enough for Crook's plans. His anxiety to escape from the man had temporarily masked his caution. He stopped at the edge of Dark Hollow, and his panting breath hid the sounds that would have warned him. He was the wrong side of the wind, and his nose told him nothing.

There was a killer hunting. He moved along the wind, silent as snowfall, never a rustle, or sibilant breath or cracked stick betraying his coming. He slipped down the hill from the blackened wood where nothing moved or grew. He loped over the grass, his body eager, his nose telling him all the news of the day. There was man-scent lying cold on the grass of the field, man-scent along with trenches that they had dug, scarring the earth, man-scent on the ground by the monsters that filled the day with horrid pounding, and filled the air with a breathtaking stink that overlaid all other scents.

There was mouse-scent, but the mouse had gone. And the scent of Uzzi, but he had gone too. And the familiar smell where Crook had walked with boots that had never been cleaned in long years. And the stale scent of Dago the lurcher cur. There was another scent, warm, alive, inviting, a saliva-bringing smell of warm body and warm fur, a clawing ache in the belly and an invitation to the tongue.

The scent lay in the wind, and came and went and came again. It lay on the grass and then it vanished, and the hunter paused, one paw lifted, sharp-muzzled head cocked on one side, fringed ears listening.

A soft breathing close by. Rik, warm, and unaware of danger, sneezed to himself softly, and Red Ruin sprang.

8

Red Ruin

Rik heard the thud of fox's pads just before Red Ruin prepared to spring. The hunter's paws slipped. In that second Rik was away, bolting for safety, erect ears sliding flat as he braced himself for flight.

The mallard, hearing the fleeing hare, woke and tissed his anger, and the drake tissed too, afraid for their babies. Red Ruin noted them. He would be back, but this time he wanted hare. He wanted to taste the sweetness, to bury his teeth in fur. He was running for his supper, and he was one large hungry ache. The hunting had been poor since the wood was burned and men came and the farm at Dark Hollow had gone. They had been careless, lazy folk at Dark Hollow Farm, their chickens and ducks and geese never safe in strong pens, but housed in ramshackle buildings that let Red Ruin in as easily as if they had not been there at all. They farmed well at Pennyplacer. Every bird was safe at night and the prowling dogs could catch the reek of fox long before he arrived. They were always ready.

Rik had a good start, and he intended to keep it that way. He could leap eight feet with ease now, his legs carrying him effortless over the ground, his sprinting bounds lifting him through the air.

Rik wanted to run uphill. He knew the way, he knew

the trail, he knew the opening through the wall, the hole in the hedge, the route across the ditch. He raced on, and fear chased behind him, ready to spring, ready to catch. He was conscious of nothing but the panting breath in his own throat and the thump of his heart, and the feel of the ground under his pads.

He ran through dry grass and over a morass where water oozed cold between his paws. He ran over tussocks that had to be cleared in one bound, avoided clinging snakey bramble stems. A furze bush bent a twig, hampering him momentarily as it caught his fur. He pulled away and sped on, leaving behind a telltale tuft that Crook found next day, and wondered about. Behind him came the relentless padding paws as Red Ruin sped after him, nose teasing out the trail, thick brush streaming, bright eyes eager, wet mouth red and ravening.

There was a brief stay at the wall. Rik ran along it, found his gap and pushed through. He jumped back again over the stones, and zig-zagged down the hill, running in long parallels, leaping from side to side, mazing the trail, dazing the fox, crazing his path, helter over the mossy clumps, skelter over the seedling furze, pelter towards the water. Run. Run. Run.

Run, avoiding the straight downhill path, for a hare will go rumble, tumble, over and over, if he runs downhill. Run and dodge, and dart away, and back on the trail, uphill again, leaping impudently over the racing fox's body, so that Red Ruin, running down, was briefly baffled and had to stop, and turn and lose ground. In that moment Rik was away, faster than speeding hawk-stoop. No chance to rest. Leap. Run. Leap sideways again and sideways. Race, and bound and spoil the trail, foil the fox and run. Dodge and dart, and jump, the long chase slowing, the two beasts faltering, the hare tiring, the fox urged on by hunger for food, hunger to kill, hunger to survive. Rik knew that terror ran behind him, even as it had with the lurcher cur, and the wicked sheepdog from Pennyplacer.

Dawn was hiding behind a cloud, its first shy light lifting the dark. There was a greying over the land, a hint of colour to come, a glimpse of the sky above, a brightness creeping over the water. The fox ran on, his pads skimming the ground. This was living, this was hunting, this was satisfaction. It was for this that he had been born.

Rik sped towards the water, zig-zagging, because the chance of an uphill rush had vanished. The water was close, a flat steely expanse, ruffled by a baby wind that played with minute waves that splashed softly, dream-like against the grass.

Paws thundered behind. The fox's breath was a rasp that clamoured on the air. The light was stronger, so that the birds in Dark Hollow woke to day, woke to see the flying beasts that fled along the Five Acre, woke to see doom running on four foxlegs while Rik bounded for his life. The sudden clamour was deafening, was terrifying, was a threat and a warning. Anger swooped from branch to branch. Anger belled on the air. Anger made tabby Tibb, who was hunting in Dark Hollow himself, pause for a moment and in that moment anger animated all the birds and they flocked together so that crow and magpie dived at Tibb's head, shouting in rage, chasing him off. He fled back to sanctuary in the old bus, raced through a hole in the side, where the metal had rusted, and jumped on to the pile of unsavoury blankets that covered Crook against the chill before the dawn, and chattered to himself in temper.

The old man, who had gone to his rest an hour before, put out a hand and stroked the cat and slowly Tibb's bushy tail flattened, his anger eased, his ruffled fur was smoothed and a slow soft purr animated every scrap of him. Dago was the fifth of a succession of lurchers and he hadn't the brains of his predecessors or the wits. No good at hunting, and never learned obedience. Crook vented his spite on the dog, making it even less likely that Dago would learn sense.

Outside, in the cold, Dago shivered on the end of his rope and turned round five times and scraped at the ground, trying to make a hollow that would shelter him from the wind that was growing to a bigger wind, and that needled him. He shivered and lay forlornly, his half-starved body huddled close, nose on paws, and slept and woke and watched for Crook coming. He was hungry. He was always hungry. He whimpered and then was quickly silent, knowing that if he woke his master the stick would fall across his back.

Day came as Rik took to the water. The fox had missed the trail, and the hare was out of sight. Rik had run and jumped until Red Ruin was dizzy. He was also so hungry that his judgement was clouded, and he was irritable with baffled rage. He could not catch the bounding, sweet-smelling creature he craved.

Rik had never tried to swim before, but swimming came by instinct and his powerful legs drove him through the water. He was making for the far side of the stream, away from the running fox, away from everything he knew. He was so small that the flooding pool seemed endless. He was crossing an inland sea, a vast stretch of water where there might be lurking perils beneath the surface.

Behind him, Red Ruin had lost all scent. The fox did not know the hare had made a truly tremendous leap to reach the water, and he did not see the small head that showed dark against the sheen, which was polished by the sun's first rays. The sun lay on the horizon, a half-ball of light, without warmth or kindness. The wind ruffled the water, and the ripples splashed eyes and nose and mouth. Rik longed for the shore.

At last there was firm ground under his pads. He bounded out and up the bank, panting. He was on new territory, quite unexplored, and he was wary. He retreated under a bush after he had shaken himself, and sat wringing the water from each ear in turn, using his two front paws. He was exhausted, and he was also hungry.

The sun began to warm the air. Rik browsed at the edge of the water, finding more succulent growth than he had ever known in the Five Acre, or in the Hawkoak Wood.

The meadow grass was long and lush and sweet as the corn in the field beyond the Hawkoak Wood. Everything on the other side of the water was tainted: by the after-reek of the smoke from the fire, by the clumsy stinking boots of the men who walked over by Five Acre, flattening the grass, grinding tiny plants beneath their heels, deep into the earth, tearing up roots as they destroyed the ground. Much of the field was bare earth, with fine hunting for Bracky as the worms lay in the surface, but poor pickings for any creature that needed fresh green herbage.

Small birds fed fat on the Five Acre, and gulls and starlings and crows invaded before the men came and after they had gone each day, finding leather-jacket and wireworm, grasshopper and beetle, woodlouse and ant. The intrusive metal grabs unearthed an ants' nest and a wasps' nest and there were fat larvae ready for the seeking beaks.

But for Rik there was nothing.

There was polythene and paper flung down carelessly after the men had eaten, and sometimes, when Rik crouched in hiding, the wind crawled into the open end of a bag and swelled it to alarming size. It filled and emptied, moving like a throbbing live thing. Once, when he went to feed after all the men had left, a sheet of newspaper, lying beyond the bulldozer, sprang into the air and met him as he turned the corner, masking his face, blinding him. He tore at it in instant panic, and left it shredded with his claws, raced for cover and lay with thumping heart for almost an hour before he dared to feed again.

Here, on the far side of the water, man had not yet come. No human boots had trampled the lush grass. No soiled paper smelled of rotting food, no grass tasted vile because of crushed cigarette ends, no clover patch was marred by the bitter dregs of tea or coffee. Here was perfection, unspoiled.

Rik bounded leisurely towards a clump of marsh clover, which he left to sample sow thistles. The stream was edged with willows. He grazed on the leaves, not long out of bud, fresh and succulent. Spring was all around him, in the sunny air of late May, in the soft haze where blue-bells covered the ground, in the clear singing yellow of an early cowslip, that dipped and shook its fragile bells. The sun dried his fur and he was warm and fed, and well content. He crouched under a whinbush, and listened to the bird notes.

A kingfisher dived from a branch, a sparkle of bright feathers, and caught a tiny fish and sat on a stone and swallowed. He had nestlings near. He flashed through the air again. The second fish was for the fledgelings, lying deep in the stinking hole that he made for them. For all his beauty his nest was a foul disgrace, and other creatures skirted it, disliking the stench of bad fish that percolated the air nearby.

The shadow vanished and the sun sweetened the air, and then from across the wide water, on the other side of the stream, came the thump of the first pump, and the harsh agony of the bulldozer engine. There were strident voices and shouts, and the din of machinery.

Rik lay in the sun and listened all day. He did not move, even when one of the apprentices came down to the stream at lunch time and sent stones skimming over the water. Rik thought the stones were meant for him. He had never seen such weapons, and did not know whether he ought to run. After a time, he realized that the stones died in the water and never reached the land, so he relaxed.

'I hate this place,' the apprentice said to a friend who came to watch him, and sat smoking, enjoying the sun on his bare chest. Rik could smell him as the wind blew across the Five Acre towards the hare.

'End of the world,' the second apprentice said. 'Not a living thing, except for a few old birds.'

He did not know that Rik crouched within earshot,

74

and that behind Rik, deep in cover, a roebuck watched, eyes and ears alert, and close to him, within a few short bounds, was the doe with twin kids, newborn: beyond them was old Bracky, who had been hunting all night, tracking home.

Among the grasses were mice and shrews and voles, a hedgehog with five young, and a squirrel, snug in her drey in the angle of a tree trunk and branch, who nursed her own babies. Everywhere, bright eyes watched the men, and the men went their way, and never saw the watchers.

When the lads had gone back to work, Rik shifted his couch, chosing to lie where the sun could bathe him in luxury. He groomed himself, combing his ears with his claws, sliding first one and then the other between his front pads, sitting erect, watchful. He heard the roebuck move, and turned his head. Briefly the two animals looked at one another, and then looked away, each knowing that the other offered no threat.

Before nightfall, Rik swam back to the Five Acre field. It was familiar, and it was home, and he knew his trails that old Crook called witch trails, and he knew the dangers that lurked there. He did not know what the night hid on the wrong side of the stream. He stopped to browse on the patch of sow thistles beside the bulldozer, but it had gone. There was only the raw scent of new-dug earth and the overlying stink of men. There was a deep open trench, the bottom of which was sticky with wet mud. He ran along the top until he tired of hunting for its end, leaped over, and galloped for the shelter of Dark Hollow. He began to graze on the grass by the stream, and in the bushes, sudden and sweet, came the carefree trill of a nightingale.

When the moon rode over the horizon and flooded the Dark Hollow with light, so that it belied its name, the bird was still singing, and the wind was sighing and there was a thrill on the air, a stir of excitement, a feeling of ease.

Rik stood on hind legs in the Dark Hollow and whirled in an ecstasy, knowing he was safe from fear for this brief moment, knowing he was alive, strong, eager and alert and coming to his prime.

He spun on his heels. He stamped and thumped, and leaped over shadowy nothings, in a crazy rhythm of his own, oblivious to all danger. The nightingale stopped singing and watched in amazement, and Hoo's two nestlings, safe in their nest, watched too, their eyes astounded. Hoo was hunting, far away downwind, and so was his mate. The young were greedy and needed filling and little that was edible had survived near their home in the hole in the high oak tree in the heart of Dark Hollow.

Rik stopped spinning. He bounded towards the water, and sat and groomed himself meticulously. He was himself again, sober and wary. He listened to the wind and the birds and, when the hunting owls returned laden, he was flat against the ground, so still that he denied his own existence.

9

Newcomers

Dog roses and honeysuckle followed the bluebells. The corn grew high, and was temptation, especially now that the machines had cleared the field and wood of all green grazing. Trenches had been dug and filled with concrete, and bricks were being laid in straight lines around them. Tip and Rik watched the peculiar behaviour of the menkind from deep in Dark Hollow. There was no place for them in the Five Acre, or in the Hawkoak Wood.

The big pumps had drained the floodwater and the stream had mysteriously vanished, carefully culverted, so that Rik could reach the grazing on the far bank without swimming. He moved distrustfully. Strangers walked over his familiar trails, and he was never sure that the patch of green on which he had fed would be there next day.

There was always something to watch. Machinery drove in and out of the field. Bricks came on big lorries, and were unloaded and stacked, and the noisy man-shouts hung in the air. Once Tip, caught by morning, crossed the edge of the Five Acre on his way back to his part of the Dark Hollow. An apprentice saw him and flung a brick which narrowly missed his head. He bounded fast for safety, and more bricks followed. Rik saw his brother race from the hurtling missiles, and both hares were careful not to appear again when men were about.

Crook Weller and his dog had also vanished. The new owners of the land would not tolerate the old man. The bus was towed away. The old poacher now lived in a Home in the nearby town and, when life became unbearable, he escaped from his bed in the dormitory, and roamed on the moors and in the fields until the police found him and brought him back. The change had so upset him that his wits wandered, and he looked for Dago, whom the Vet had put to sleep, and for tabby Tibb, who had escaped, and was living wild, fed by the men on the building site, who saw the old cat straying and felt sorry for him.

The hares knew none of this. They only knew that the lurcher cur had ceased to plague them, and that the man was never to be seen at night. The night was theirs, and only the wild things owned it. The owl and the barking fox, and stoat and weasel. And sometimes Tibb, who was a splendid hunter.

One bright morning in July, Tibb had been prowling after the most delectable smell in the whole world, hunting along the wind, looking for a mate. He found her in the farmyard at Pennyplacer. He found two other tomcats there, and battled with them, making such a din that the farmer emptied a bucket of water over them. The battle was resumed later, and Tibb was victor. He took up residence in the haystack, where he could shelter from the wind and wet, and the farmer left him there, as he soon discovered that where Tibb lived, the rats died, and Tibb paid far more than a fair rent. Every day at least five corpses lay in the yard, put side by side for the farmer to see.

Before many weeks had passed, there were four new kittens on the farm, and Tibb belonged, with a saucer of frothing milk as his reward. He grew fatter than ever before, and forgot Crook Weller, but the old man did not forget him, and whenever he saw a tabby cat, he went to it and stroked it, hoping it was his. But it never was.

There was still much for Rik to learn. The houses grew, day by day, until they towered high, and men used ladders to work on the roofs, and bricks were succeeded by tiles. The open gaps, through which Rik and Tip had often run at night, were closed by doors. Glass panes filled the windows, and reflected strange lights that moved and glittered and puzzled the two hares, who often saw the reflections bend and twist and glint when the moon was high.

There was no longer even a memory of Five Acre or of Hawkoak Wood. There were houses and streets, and then came the first family, moving in as soon as the house was built, hanging curtains in the windows, putting strange objects on the sills, and building a small wall that did not keep out a hare, but did enclose a garden that was dug and sown with grass. The new grass was sweeter than the corn in the field, and Rik and Tip kept it well clipped down to ground level, until the owners of the house pegged nets over it to keep off birds and beasts and hung strings on which were brilliant dangling lengths of foil that glittered and rustled frighteningly in the wind. The two young hares avoided the garden. The house occupants warned their neighbours about the wild

things that destroyed young shoots, and the newcomers all took precautions, so that there was no grazing for the hares, who returned to the cornfield.

Summer flared to beauty, flowers in every hedge and flowers in Dark Hollow. The men worked, shirtless, revelling in the sun, their bodies tanned and glowing. Summer brought honeysuckle, and big bumble bees that burred cosily among the flowers : it brought vivid scents that masked the warning reek of Weh and Starra, and that caused the death of many little beasts.

There were newcomers too. The men left their food lying on the ground, and not only the birds fed well. The rats came, knowing by some instinct that where man was would be rubbish on which they might feed fat. They thrived on garbage that no other beasts would touch, they made nests under the garden walls, they bred, and their babies grew and foraged round the houses. The house-holders liked to feed the birds. They did not know they were feeding the rats, and that anything that lay on the ground at night went into rat bellies. The sharp noses and bright eyes were a hand's throw from the people, but they were never seen.

Until one of them became too bold and went in through an open door, smelling food. He was seen by the owner of the house who bought a cat. A big, vicious tomcat, that had been picked up by the R.S.P.C.A. Ginger began his own war on rat and rabbit, and one dark night, prowling along the ditch, he met Weh the weasel, slipping back to his old hunting ground in Dark Hollow.

Ginger and Weh fought a battle that was heard by every creature for many hundred yards. Spit and hiss and fear scream, and the sound of Weh dying, made Rik shiver into the ground, lying flatter than a fallen leaf, blending into nothing. Beyond him, the roebuck family, also now living in Dark Hollow, huddled one against the other, and listened.

Ginger carried his trophy home in triumph. He jumped through the kitchen window, and laid it on the mat, as a thank offering to his owners. He could not understand the fuss the next morning when his mistress found a dead weasel under the kitchen table. Her screams of appalled horror woke all the beasts in the Dark Hollow, who listened, unable to tell what wild animal was making such a noise.

The weasel was buried and Ginger was scolded. He did not know what he had done wrong, but next night, when he tried to get into the house, a rat hanging from his jaws, he found the window closed against him, and went to look for a shelter out of the rain. He found it in a coal house and, next day, came more trouble, because his paws marked a white bedspread on which he sought comfort after a distinctly lumpy night.

His new owners regretted having bought a cat but, as he kept the rats down, he was given a small kennel outside the house, where he could shelter, and from this he waged war on every beast that ran, and Rik learned that Ginger was as much to be feared as Weh had been, and that whenever tabby Tibb or this newcomer appeared, it was time for him to vanish.

10

The Hunt

Rik had lived through spring and summer : he had seen
his homeplace change. He had seen many of his trails
vanish, built over, replaced by houses. He had seen the
Hawkoak Wood wounded by the Great Wind and killed
by the fire. He had seen the water that he had swum
across disappear, and the stream vanish. He had watched
men come to the quiet places, and their noises replace
the sound of the wind in the trees. He had seen the trees
go away on big lorries.

He was now full-grown, though his body was not yet
as well-muscled as it would be in another year's time. He
was larger than tabby Tibb, fully as large as Ginger and,
when he stretched on his hind legs to reach the ears of
growing corn, and to pull them down with his two front
paws, he was almost three feet tall.

His dense coat of yellowy brown had darker markings
on back and ears and tail. His underparts were white.
His sensitive ears lent expression to his oval head, and his
large brown eyes were always glowing with life. His
underfur was so close and thick that only the worst of
rainstorms wetted him to the skin, and he kept himself as
clean as any cat. Wariness was his guardian, and ears
and eyes and nose all worked together to keep him safe.

The Dark Hollow was now his home, and his ways

had changed. His trails led not to the Hawkoak Wood and the Five Acre field, but to the cornfield at Penny-placer, to the grazing on the other side of the culverted stream, as yet untouched by the builders, to the garden at Dark Hollow Farm, which had also escaped man's intrusive hands. Here, without men to tend it, the plants ran riot, and Rik browsed on tall-growing, sharp-tasting ferny fronds of parsley, on dandelions that seeded thickly in every corner, on a spreading of dahlias and of carnations, all overgrown by weeds. In the far corner lettuce had bolted and here was rich feeding indeed, and here one night he met Tip for the first time for weeks.

Tip was as big as Rik, but less wary. He faced his brother over the parsley heads and, suddenly irate, he boxed at Rik, who boxed back in anger. A moment later and they were fighting in earnest, no longer brother and brother, but two male hares who might be rivals. Rik turned and lashed out with his hind legs and Tip, caught off guard, rolled over and ran. Rik chased him out of the garden and returned to the parsley and fed until he could hold no more.

Tip returned to the cornfield.

The days were shortening again, with summer over. The leaves, weary with dust, were darkening to autumn glow. The grass itself was tired and strawlike and the corn was ripe and ready for cutting, though Tip did not know that. He finished feeding, and settled down near the corncrake's nest, safe hidden among the long stems that bowed in the wind. He had spent most of his time in the field, and the farmer at Pennyplacer had sworn to get him. He had done too much damage, feeding night after night.

By now the hares were used to the sound of machinery, as were all the other animals, so that Tip merely lay close when the big combine harvester came into the field.

It began to cut.

The blades worked along the edge of the field. The harvester drove round and round, each circle smaller than the last, the spilled golden ears picked over by birds that flew in behind, finding rich gleanings.

Tip, discovering that the big machine was coming closer and closer to his resting place, slid off through the corn, ears well back on his head, moving cautiously, anxious not to be seen. He was so slow that no one caught a glimpse of him, and not a stalk of corn betrayed his passing. He settled in the centre of the field, where mice hid and two hedgehogs trembled, and five young rabbits crouched in fear.

Round again came the scything blades, moving in, closer and closer, until there was only a last small patch of unreaped corn.

The blades scythed the edge, too close for comfort, and one of the rabbits bolted and reached the ditch and was away, pursued by the demons of fear, but by nothing else.

The second rabbit sped for safety, and Tip could stay no longer. He saw the blades glint in the sun and, in his turn, ran. The farmer was waiting. The gun spoke and Tip rolled and died, and another gun took the rabbit that had chased beside him.

Deep in Dark Hollow, Rik heard the guns but he did not know their message. He cuddled down in the scrape he had hollowed in the ground, and listened to the song of the big harvester as it cut the last of the standing corn. He was the only one of Kee's litter to survive. He shared

Dark Hollow with the roebuck family and the hedgehogs and, at times, with Red Ruin, who had an earth there. Starra spent his time near the haystacks at Pennyplacer, hunting vermin. The hedgehogs moved about the gardens and helped the big ginger tom dispose of the rats that plagued the houses. They came for scraps flung to the birds, and put on the compost heaps, and dropped by the dustbins. Nobody in the houses saw the hedgehogs.

Nobody knew that Red Ruin came at night to see what he could find, or that Rik sometimes hopped through the gardens in the darkness and stared up at the lights in the houses. He lurked in the new planted bushes that had begun to give cover for small creatures, and stared, astounded, through the open curtains at the strange antics of the people who occupied the rooms.

Sometimes a cat sat on a window ledge, gazing into the night, and chattered his teeth at the hare, but no one understood him. Once a dog barked, seeing movement near the gate, and a woman cuffed the animal and drew the curtains, and left the windows blind. Rik nibbled at a pansy planted near a gate, and loped back to Dark Hollow, where few people ever came, and the children were forbidden to play, because of the treachery of the deep pool, which could drown them. They had other interests. Few of them cared for the country pleasures that lay almost at their doors. They had all come from the city, and found the country too quiet.

The country was all around them, even if they did not wish to know. The estate was surrounded by farmland, and there were moors and woods and fields to the west of Dark Hollow. The builders had not yet started on the farmland, and the country people had their own amusements to pass the autumn days, amusements that were as alien to the people in the houses as they were to Rik, who became involved in them.

He was aware of change, this time in the air, not in the world around him. There was a sharpness each morning and needling chill, and sometimes there was hoarfrost on the ground, a mere sugar sprinkling, that numbed his paws. At times mist seeped up from the water and hid the trees, and the centre of Dark Hollow was isolated, mysterious, remote, a haunted place that might have lain a million miles from man. Man noises came to it, muffled by the fog. The early morning noises were now part of Rik's life. The clatter of milk bottles, the rattle of letterboxes as newspapers and post were delivered, the laughter and taunts and teasing jeers of the children on their way to school.

September had come with a warmth in the days and a chill in the nights, and the grass was not so tasty. Rik began to browse on whitethorn bark and to raid the furrows at Pennyplacer for turnips, which he skinned and ate untidily, betraying himself, and swedes and mangolds. He was always hungry.

With October came big winds again, but none like the Great Wind, which had been the worst gale known to man in living memory—and that went back almost one hundred years, for old Jo Biggin, the great grandfather of the children at Pennyplacer, had been born when Victoria was on the throne, and he could remember events from long before 1900 vividly.

One October morning, before the people on the estate had left their beds, a man came to Dark Hollow. He looked about until he found the earth where Red Ruin

sometimes lay, and he stopped it with stake and stick
and made it safe. Red Ruin could not enter. Rik, lying in
the dying bracken, hidden from sight, watched curious-
ly. Men were always doing something that was beyond
all understanding. He ignored them, so long as they did
not come too near, or throw sticks or stones or gunshot
at him.

The man went away. Rik had fed all night and was
drowsy. He listened, and sniffed the morning air, which
was sharp with frost, so that his breath hung in small
clouds in front of his face. This was something that he
had not seen before, and he was puzzled, but in time he
grew used to it and ignored it. Once he pawed at the
little cloud as if it were tangible and then he cuddled
closer to keep warm.

There was a faint blue sky above him, and a trace of
sunshine that lacked all comfort. His quick ears heard a
car as it changed gear far away, and then his body felt
the earth tremble beneath him. He sat erect, alert, his
eyes scanning Dark Hollow. Nothing moved. The water
bubbled clear and cold, the grass bent in the wind and
the dying fox-red bracken shivered under the rustling
trees.

The trembling was a shaking in the ground, and
above it there were noises. Thunderous, unknown and
unidentifiable noises, a stampeding, a million hoarse
throats baying, shouting, pounding, thumping, thudding. The din came closer, turned aside, and drew away
and then was closer still.

There was fear on the air, there was terror, there was
panic, and then, bewilderingly, there was Red Ruin
running for his life and Red Ruin never ran from any-

thing that Rik knew. If the fox was running there was danger, there was death, and the sudden birdcalls confirmed it.

They didn't speak of the running fox. They called, sharp and urgent. Danger. Danger. Red Ruin came speeding through Dark Hollow, ears flat on his head, tail streaming, breath panting harsh in his throat, heart thudding. Rik dived across the Hollow to the other side of the water and was ready, in his turn, to bolt.

The fox reached his earth. He stared at it in disbelief. His red brush drooped. He could not believe his eyes. Then, as the first hound thrust through the undergrowth, Red Ruin turned and ran. There was nowhere to go. Nowhere to hide. There was nothing left but to run until his heart burst with running, or the hounds caught him, or he found new sanctuary. His last retreat was blocked.

There was pandemonium in the wood.

Bird noise was urgent, and birds flapped and flew from tree to tree. The spill of hounds was everywhere, sterns waving, eager noses hard on the trail, as each traced the scent. Red Ruin had left a good line behind him. Ravager and Ransom, Painter and Peel, Captain and Major Duke and Darkness, each fled along the telltale track, chasing the flying fox.

Behind them, less certain, learning their trade, came the new entry. Pelham and Pavlo, Tango and Teal, chasing after their fellows, enjoying themselves immensely, but not working at all, so that as the Huntsman came up to them he was annoyed and tried to teach them their business.

He was out of luck, because Pelham had scented Rik. A moment later, the turmoil was intense, as the horses galloped into what was left of the wood. The older hounds ran straight and true after Red Ruin but Rik panicked and bolted from cover, towards the main body of the Hunt.

He leaped two hounds and turned aside, twisting between stamping ironshod hooves. Men reined in their horses, cursing, and the horses shied and reared and whinnied, as the four young hounds turned back after the hare and were in danger of being trampled.

Rik was out of Dark Hollow, racing along the muddy road that had not yet been finished. There was a wide ditch at the end and he leaped it, and ran on, and behind him came the four hounds, quite beyond control, and the horses pounded after, not sure what had happened to the rest of the Hunt but determined to have some fun.

Across the streets Rik ran, and between the houses, with children running to look. Over the gardens, leaping the low fences, following, to the best of his ability, the old vanished trails that he had once known so well.

He doubled back on his tracks, retracing his own path, and the baffled hounds hunted about, and lost the scent. Rik lay close, under a garden shed that was mounted on two runners, leaving a gap beneath. He did not move until the moon was high, and all sound had ceased.

Behind him, in the wood, the Hunt had sorted itself out and followed after the fox. Red Ruin knew the hounds were almost on him, were at his heels, were reaching for his brush. He was ready to turn and fight, to use tooth and claw and snapping jaws, to inflict vicious bite and raking scratch before he died. He was a gallant fighter. He came out into the road between the houses and, in his turn, fled along the path, turning in through a gate.

There was a garden wall, and he jumped onto it and ran along. There was the roof of a shed, beneath which Rik was cowering. Red Ruin jumped on top. There was the kitchen roof, an outbuilding, easy to gain, and he was on top, and jumping again for the slope of a porch, and again, and he was on the house roof, two stories up, lying against the chimney, looking down, and the milling hounds were baying, the men were cursing and the jostling horses were turning and tramping, their hooves a-clatter on the hard macadam.

Red Ruin lay on the roof, recovering his breath. No one could reach him. The houseowners did not approve of hunting and refused to allow anyone to climb a ladder and dislodge the fox. One hour, and then another passed, and the Hunt went home to tea, and the hounds back to their kennels, and the horses to grooming and food and a warm stable or chilly field.

A reporter arrived and photographed the sharp foxface that peered down from the rooftop, and Red Ruin was briefly famous next day, as everyone read of the fox on the rooftop and thought it extraordinary that he should have run among houses, and sought sanctuary there. Not even the Huntsmen realized that the fox had run along his old trail, which skirted the Five Acre field and ended in Hawkoak Wood, and that the house on which he sought refuge was directly above his favourite earth, under an old elm that had died in the fire. His feet had led him unerringly, in spite of the houses that now covered the ground.

Midnight was two hours gone when Red Ruin crept

down, jumping from roof to roof again until he gained the wall and the ground. He could smell Rik, but was too tired to hunt. He made his way to Pennyplacer and, after resting, foraged for rats. Then, as dawn was announcing the new day, he left the area for good, and loped off through field and wood and hollow, until he came to a wide expanse of peaty moor where he could lie in peace. He never returned to his old haunts, and Rik had one enemy less to fear.

The first milkcart was rattling along the road when Rik crept out of his own hiding place, and loped behind the walls, unseen. He stopped often, smelling the air, but it was tainted with petrol fumes and told him little but that there were many cars about. He had been badly frightened by the hounds, and when a dog scented him and heard his stealthy movements and barked, Rik arrowed over the wall, almost under the wheels of the passing milkcart. He missed the wheels and sped on, until he was safe in the heart of Dark Hollow, cuddled close in his own form, listening to the birds as they greeted the day.

11

Snow

October was wild and wet and windy, and Rik spent much of it in Dark Hollow. He had learned to come out much later than usual, when men were safe in their houses, and the windows were black. Once the last light had vanished, almost all movements ceased in the streets. Before then, there was danger. One man owned a young greyhound, which twice had roused Rik from his form and sent him dashing for safety. The greyhound was not yet old enough to be a menace, but his day would come.

The houses close to Dark Hollow were completed. Those who lived near to it disliked the trees and bushes, and the feeling of wildness within its small space. It was a tiny island of green in the midst of a desert where nothing grew.

Rik watched the new streets made, and vans come and the furniture move in. He watched children ride their tricycles in the street, unaware that only a few yards from them, the hare lay close, intrigued by their activities. He learned to avoid cars, but at night, if he was caught in the headlights, he was bewildered and blinded, and owed his life to the fact that those who had seen him had not wished him harm, and had been driving slowly.

There were twelve houses now occupied and more

being built. The noise of the builders dominated each day.

November was rainy, and the parts of the estate which were not yet finished became a morass. The stream thrust angrily through the culvert, and at one point burst out, as no one had realized how fast it could flow when filled with rain from the hills, which were so far away that men forgot them. A big pump was installed and the thump and thud of its engine intrigued Rik who often went to look at it at night, excited by the tremor in the ground beneath him.

December brought a new danger. There were no leaves on the trees, or the bushes, and the Dark Hollow was a dismal, sodden place, open to view. The grass was dry and dead and stringy. The builders had moved on to the old farm, and were destroying the garden, and Rik had to widen his explorations, as food was scarce. Not even the planted gardens could help him now.

He ate moss, and he ate bark. In one of the new gardens there was a willow tree, just planted, and the bark was sweet. Rik browsed at night, and his long tracks in the earth were plainly visible. The owner of the willow tree, finding that it was dying, asked a naturalist friend to come and give an opinion.

That was easy.

'Hare,' the man said, and went to look in Dark Hollow, where he found that Rik had scraped himself a long shallow hole in which to shelter, and left other telltales. There was no sign of Rik himself. He heard the two men coming, feeling their footsteps shake the ground, which vibrated under his body. He loped off, ears flat, and was hidden behind a small wall, protected by the side of a shed which stood close against it. He listened, and when the men had gone, he went back to Dark Hollow, but dug himself a new scrape on the other side of the stream, not liking the stink of tobacco they had left behind, or the dottle from a pipe that had been knocked out beside his recently vacated form.

That day, although Rik did not know it, work was begun on another scheme that was to change the area entirely. The ground beyond Pennyplacer was levelled for a new airport that would bring planes from all over the world. The farmer at Pennyplacer had hung on for as long as he could. He had hoped that the petition against the airport would ensure that the building never took place, but now he in his turn would have to go, and Pennyplacer was destined to follow Dark Hollow Farm into memory.

One day, just before Christmas, the big vans came and took away furniture and farm implements, sheep and cattle, the dog and Grey Cat, and tabby Tibb. They had been lucky to find another farm in Wales, and were going for ever. Rik, who had been browsing in the grass at the edge of the cornfield, watched them go. For the next few weeks he had the entire farm to himself, and fed well again. The grass was thin and winter was starving the land, but there were no other hares to take his food. The roebuck and his family had joined Bracky in the West Wood, as there was no more cover in Dark Hollow.

Christmas came, with a sugarfrost of snow, with bright coloured lights in the houses that sparked on and off, and that intrigued Rik, who spent many hours watching them, lying in the dark within the shelter of a wall that shielded him from the icy wind. Warmth was far away, forgotten. He could not even remember how it felt.

Sometimes at night he huddled against a chimney breast, feeling the heat from the brickwork, but the slightest unusual noise sent him pelting for safety. He had known the smell and sound of Weh and Starra, and of Red Ruin. He knew the diving shadow of hawk and owl and kestrel, but men were totally unpredictable. They might ignore him, or stone him, or shoot at him. They might fail to see him, or point at him and laugh, or they might set dogs on him. He could never be sure. So all were treated alike, as enemies, to be hated and feared. A ghost of man-smell, a sound of man-feet, and Rik was away, trusting no one.

Christmas brought more mystery, for people visited one another, driving from house to house. Children and parties of grown-ups walked the streets in the dark, and the sound of carols rose above the constant keening of the wind, and Rik listened, liking the rhythm and the music. Sometimes he was only a short distance away, ready to bolt if disturbed, watching and listening, interested in the antics of the two-legged creatures that lived in the buildings.

Christmas Day dawned with a carillon of midnight bells, ringing a peal from the church, clear and sweet on the icy air. The plunging notes were a call to Rik, a call that he did not understand, but that excited him, and when the moon flung her light in the Hollow, he spun on his heels, dancing, twisting, twirling, whirling, ears flat against his head, lost in an intense ecstasy of rapid movement that only stopped when his head was spinning too.

That night snow fell, and Rik watched, puzzled. He had never seen snow before. He brushed the thick clinging flakes from fur and nose and eyes and whiskers, but

more came and at last he huddled close against the ground in one of his scrapes and his warm body melted the snow around him so that he lay in a hole, surrounded by low white cliffs that he nosed, and shied away from. Snow fell all night, and in the morning Rik was a sharp darkness, plain for everyone to see, and children, walking to church, saw him and pointed. He loped off, sinking in at every bound.

He reached the stream and found that that too had vanished and, instead of running water, was covered in a hard glisten that betrayed his paws so that he slid when he ventured on to the surface. He crossed to the other side, loped over a small hill that hid him from the houses, and dug through the snow until he found the sparse food that kept him alive. He was still hungry when he had fed, and he went to the willow and stripped the bark.

Daytime brought children to the Dark Hollow, where they played in the snow. Three boys built a snowman against the trunk of a tree, and Rik, encountering it later, and smelling the boy-smell that was quite unlike man-smell, backed away. Then, curious, he sniffed round it in a circle and stared up at it, towering above him, its snowy body already beginning to thaw, two stones for eyes slipping out of place, the old stick in its mouth falling with a plop that startled him so that he bounded away, and turned back again to eye the hat that sat so jauntily on the shapeless head. Nightly, it became smaller and smaller, until at last the only reminder was the boy-smell that remained on the ground.

Children slid along the frozen stream. One of them went through the ice and into the water, which was, fortunately, only a few inches deep, but it was bitterly cold and she went home yelling. The noise she made sent Rik away, stealing out of Dark Hollow, through the gardens, back to Pennyplacer.

He had not been there for some days, and that too had begun to alter. The builders planned to pull down the farmhouse as soon as the holiday ended, and the now familiar machinery was already in place. Tabby Tibb was there too. He had gone away with the farmer, but had been frightened of the lorry in which he was travelling and, as they stopped at traffic lights only a mile away, he had clawed his way out of his basket, jumped down, and gone back to the place he knew. There were plenty of rats to eat, and there were mice and a few young rabbits, and birds. And there were always people. Tibb knew that if he arrived at a back door and sat there, purring loudly, one ear drooping, a pleading expression in his green eyes, he would most certainly receive a saucer of milk, or a scrap of meat. Meanwhile he slept in a deserted barn, snug in the hay. When he went down the hill to the houses, he fought battle after battle with Ginger, and the two inflicted many scars on one another, but neither ever won.

Rik smelled Tibb, and knew that an enemy had come back to the farm. Life had been very peaceful. A moment later, he was away as Starra came prowling, having remembered the rats and come to look for them in one of his favourite places. Rik sped over the ground, back along the roads and through the gardens, until he came to Dark Hollow. But that was no longer sanctuary. The children had left paper, ice cream cartons and rubbish everywhere, and the smell of them caught in his throat. He crouched in the thawing snow, uneasy and uncomfortable, and winter-wild hunger gnawed at him. Life had changed beyond all recognition. His horizon was narrowed to bricks and mortar, to hard roads and bleak trees.

Rik lay with his nose on his paws and his ears flat, and endured. He clung to life, but it lacked all savour, and hunger became near starvation.

It seemed to be the end of his world. He did not know that winter would end and spring bring warmth again. He only knew he was cold and hungry and that he suffered.

12

Hunger!

January that year was bitter cold. Icy winds blew constantly from the north and, when the air warmed, snow followed and lay deep. Rik raided the gardens, and browsed on the farm stubble at Pennyplacer. The builders could not work. The ground was too hard and it was far too cold.

This respite saved several animals that might have died. There were bales of hay and an odd sack of corn which enabled mice and rats to eat, and these kept tabby Tibb fat.

Hunger! It stalked among every living creature in the wild. Some of the birds fed on bread in the gardens, some of them found that people put out wild bird seed on the bird tables. One house had three bird tables and three feeders full of nuts, and here came thrush and blackbird and greenfinch, coaltit and bluetit and great tit, robin and wren, and a multitude of sparrows and starlings. Here too came fieldfares, brought in from the frozen fields by the news of food, and a missel thrush, a rare visitor, and two wood pigeons, who sat in the trees and rewarded their hosts with their constant soft musical crooning. The birds had survived the summer and all of them were wary. Ginger stalked them without success, day after day, and they flew off safely. As soon as he came, the sentinel starling cried his chirring, rattling warning, and the garden emptied.

Hunger! It turned Starra the stoat into a prowling wickedness, savage for food, so that one night he killed a kitten that had stayed out too late, and another he fought a game battle with Ginger. Neither animal won, and Starra returned to Pennyplacer, so sore that, while he was licking his wounds, he failed to see Tibb. Tibb had grown strong and wily and was as dangerous as a wildcat in the Highlands. There was a brief moment of realization, and then darkness came for the stoat, and his world was lost for ever.

Hunger! It was a January spectre, a prowling angry ghost, a haunting horror that left little creatures dead for want of food. It was torture, it was torment, it was a twisting ache that was never soothed, that cried for food and more food, that hunted fruitlessly along the furrows, that pulled bark from the winter-stark trees, that nibbled the minute leaf buds that had not yet begun to swell with life. It was a stilling in the night, a solitary dying, a shivering and a shaking, a fluffing of feathers, a thinning of little bodies that yearned for the sun to bring back bounty. None of them had known such hardship before, for there had been the two farms and the wood, and the Five Acre field, and there all had found enough to tide over the lean days.

There had been berries on the bushes and many small creatures lurking in the dead leaves that covered the ground thickly, and kept out the wind. There had been moss and grasses and the nuts that the squirrel had hoarded and forgotten, and the stores set apart by thrifty fieldmice. There had been shining russet-bronze chestnuts for many creatures to nibble, for none despised seeds when there was no meat to be found.

Now there was nothing. There was only the harsh keening of the wind and the creak of freezing trees, the crackle as the pool beneath the willows in Dark Hollow froze. There was the whisper of rain on the snow and the cruel bite of ice when the showers ended. There was the endless cold of night, and the brief light that came from dawn to dusk.

Hunger! Even when he slept Rik knew he was empty, and woke and tried forlornly to find grazing under the snow, and hastened up the hill, loping along the hard streets, the surface slippery under his feet as he went to find food at Pennyplacer, and foraged forlornly in the hay, only a few feet away from the roebuck family, who came there nightly, seeking fodder for life.

January ended and February came with a thaw and a flood that spread from the spring in the Dark Hollow, and through the streets and the new estate. Houses were flooded inches deep in icy water, the fire engines and the pumps came back, and Rik fled from Dark Hollow, swimming part of the way, coming out chilled and aching, to creep forlornly into a deserted shed at Penny-placer, and lie shivering among fusty sacks to dry himself, knowing by instinct that he must keep out of the wind, though he was unaware it would freeze the water on his fur, and kill him with cold.

The floods passed and the builders returned to Penny-placer. There, too, the grazing vanished, faster than before, as the men were working against time, with high payments for speedy completion. There was nothing left for any of the creatures at Pennyplacer. The roebuck family were the first to go and find sanctuary in West Wood, which was not yet destined to become part of the town.

The children had found Dark Hollow in the winter, and now they began to haunt it. They were not country trained. They tore up flowers by the roots, they pulled branches from the trees, they left rubbish everywhere. More rubbish came. The people in the houses brought out all kinds of things to tip into the stream, or drop into the pool. Old bicycles and a rusty and battered car, without seats or engine or headlamps, were flung carelessly, to be hidden, fouling the water. Old mattresses and corsets, unsightly derelict prams, bits of corrugated iron, sodden decaying paper, a bale of mouldy straw, which a child had bought for his rabbit and had discovered to be unfit, and a multitude of other unlikely objects accumulated in the wood and, as the year grew to summer, were overgrown, and became hidden traps for the unwary.

One Sunday three boys set up a row of milk bottles and smashed them with stones so that the sharp shards lay in the new grass. Rik, bounding towards his form near the willows, cut his paw to the bone. He limped into cover and licked at the wound. It was very sore.

He could no longer race for safety. He couched in the growing brambles, and fed on the grass that was beginning to show green again. He was sick and tired, and hunger was not so urgent. The wound healed cleanly, but remained to plague him for days and, when he began to move more freely, the injured leg ached, and his movements were not so certain.

There was nowhere left to feed but in the gardens. He browsed among plants that were beginning to bud,

and so angered the man with the greyhound, that, one Sunday morning, before anyone was up, he brought the dog out, and sent it into Dark Hollow.

Rik knew that he should run for cover. Greyhounds were swift, and hares were their common prey, and long instinct had taught him, but there was no cover left. He could only rely on speed and cunning. He fled beyond the willows, out onto the road, and vanished, a moment later, over a wall. The dog could not follow. He in his turn, had fallen victim to the spears of glass. He limped back to his master, his leg bleeding copiously from a cut that had almost sawn off a pad, and he spent the rest of the morning at the Vet, having stitches in the wound and a penicillin injection. He was carried home. The family valued him, and he lay in state by the fire and fed on chicken when the family ate their Sunday lunch. He so enjoyed the fuss that for years afterwards, whenever he felt in need of more affection than usual, he walked on three legs, holding up a pathetic paw and the family said :

'Poor old boy. Does it hurt then?'

The greyhound would wag a frantic tail, and the children would laugh because he had forgotten which leg had been hurt and held up the wrong one.

Long after the dog had gone, Rik continued to run. He ran along the hard road, bounding out of the path of speeding cars, and once almost lost his life as a big sports car came fast round a corner. It missed him by a fraction of an inch and he went on, more slowly, his lame leg aching. He wanted green grass, and growing things, and earth under his paws, and the clean country fields. There was a reminder of trees on the wind, and he followed it, smelling, for the first time for months, the scent of growing flowers, of buds on branches, and of woodland.

He came to the West Wood at sunset, and bounded warily down one of the firebreaks. West Wood was man-made, a new plantation where once there had been natural forest. It smelled of man. Rik dug himself a long scrape near a big tree, sheltered from the wind by a hummock that, if he had been able to see into the ground, would have shown him that it hid old Bracky.

When the nightwind danced in the budding branches, Rik began to feed. He found young buds and bark, and thin grass, and sprouting leaves and, for the first time for weeks, the ache inside him was appeased, and he rested, totally content. The wind that stole between the swaying trunks was alive with the rumour of spring, with the promise of warmth to come, with memories of summer. It was the last day of February. March was almost here. As yet, Rik did not know about March, but he did know that inside him was a wild stirring, a feeling that he had never experienced before, a beginning of exhilaration, a need that had to be satisfied. There was, in the wind, on the air, all round him, a heady scent that called him, and that, when he had rested, he would have to follow, no matter where it led.

Meanwhile, he cuddled close against the ground, his ears flat, his wide eyes watching, and panted softly. Warm for the first time for months, he sneezed, and a woodmouse, wandering nearby, scuttled into a crack in a tree trunk, his small heart thumping in terror.

Rik began to groom himself, cleaning his ears and face, paying especial attention to the new-healed cut on his leg, over which the fur was just beginning to grow.

The air was astir with excitement now. He would have to find out the cause. He sat erect, sniffing, identifying all the sounds and all the smells that he knew. But this was different. This was invitation. This was the beginning of delirium. He began to spin, all by himself in the dark wood, just before the day, his paws thumping on the ground. Below him, Bracky grunted angrily at the tremor in the ground, and turned around and went to sleep again.

When dawn came in a sudden triumph of light, Rik was still dancing. He had become a mad March hare, but why, he did not know.

13

March Hare

March was the wild hares dancing.

March was the new-turned furrows, the earth rich and dark.

March was a tint of green on the withered grass and a blackbird singing. It was last year's brittle ragwort and sorrel, and time-wrecked bracken. It was twiggy hedges, tangled with grey straggles of old man's beard. It was water, running free, new released from ice-thrall, and pools in which the reflected trees were black images against a steely ground. It was chestnut sheen of fattening buds on the trees and lambs lying under the pussy willows.

March was nesting birds and the flare and flirt of bright courtship among the bushes. It was flaunting magpies, bowing and dipping, the sheen on their wings peacock blue in the sunlight, the sudden frisk of long tails expressive as spoken word.

March was promise.

March was knobby black seedheads, their bounty long forgotten. It was crisp rustle of sere brown leaves clinging obstinately to the beech hedges. It was the swift stoop of the peregrine, busy catching nothing as he sought to impress his mate with his prowess.

March was a sudden flash of aconites, a gleam of gold

from early celandines in sheltered hollows. March was a softening of stark outlines of the storm-marked trees.

March was the high winds flattening the strawy grass, was a skelter of white cloud across a blue sky, was a pattern of birdsong. When the gales shrieked over the hummocks and the windshout was all around them, the dancing hares whirled faster and beat the ground and brindled with excitement.

March was one week old when Rik joined them.

He had spent that day in a hollow scrape at the edge of West Wood. He was aware of the movements of the roebuck family behind him, as they foraged for food. The last year's kids were now as old as he and, a few months later, there would be new kids born to the doe. Meanwhile the buck watched over his family, and his quick bark and drumming hooves alerted all of them.

The roebuck vanished as if they had never been. Rik flattened himself against the ground, hidden perfectly from all but the quickest eyes. The man walking beneath the trees, taking a short cut to the main road, saw none of them and, when he had gone, the quiet wood was alive again, as the creatures stirred and left their hiding places.

Dusk came fast, with batflit and owlcall, and with the dusk came urgency. Rik had sat on his hind legs and sniffed the wind. The last shadows fled across the ground, hurrying in the wake of clouds that masked the moon. Rik, looking up, saw that the moon was a ghost of herself, a faint reflection, no more. The clouds parted, and mysteriously, came total darkness, as the ghost moon was slowly swallowed. The effect was uncanny and the animals crouched and waited for light. They did not know that the moon was in eclipse. They only knew that something unusual had occurred.

The light crept back, and the shadows danced again beneath the trees. The wind flew towards Rik, ruffling his fur, teasing his nose, bringing news.

He whirled, twisting and spinning under the trees. He was excitement, he was life, he was mazy with delight. He slowed, stopped, and began to graze, but the news that the wind brought would not let him eat. He followed the call that was strong, insistent.

Lope along the high road, and read the wind. Sit, sniff and hurry on, through silent sleeping gardens, past shuttered houses, across the deserted motorway into the fields beyond. Now he was on new ground, on foreign land, among unknown enemies, but he had forgotten caution. The scent in his nostrils drowned all other scents, but he was protected by the fates that watch over the unwary at such times. He loped on.

Over the moor, where Red Ruin now lived, skirting the new gash that would soon be a runway for jet planes from all over the world, and into the meadows that bounded it, and would soon be part of the airfield.

The scent, stronger now, was all around him. It lay on the grass, it flew on the air, it called him over and over. He did not yet know its source but, as he came to the edge of the meadow, he saw other hares. There were ten of them, and among them was his own mother Kee, who had long forgotten about him, and a little brown hare with docile eyes who watched as the bucks danced, in a dizzy file, twisting and spinning as Rik had spun beneath the trees in the West Wood.

He had to join in. He had to follow. He had no choice.

March was here, with a roar of wind and a surge of rain that flurried from the sky and vanished again, unnoticed. The Jack hares stamped and twisted, round and round, to and fro, in a crazy, mazy, dazing dance that had a rhythm of its own, a tremendous urgency that mastered all of them, that caused each to try to excel, jumping higher than the rest, bounding one over another, chasing, racing, leaping, while Kee and the little doe watched and waited.

The moon came out again and shone on the whirling hares. Dance and leap, twist and spin. Whirl and wheel, dart and turn. Lope, and follow in single file, along the meadow edge, over the dark new-ploughed furrows, glistening wet in the rain, leap and lope and keep in line. Leap and lope back to the meadow where the does sit waiting, grazing on sweet green clover, watching with dark eyes glowing.

The thrilling hirr-birr was stronger now, was mastering all of them, so that in their antics they ignored the does, forgot why they danced and leaped and spun under the golden moon, forgot everything in the world but the feelings inside them. The night wore on. They followed one another until the sun's light broke the darkness and flooded the meadow. Then one and another moved away. Kee and the doe had both vanished to their own forms, slipping away unseen while the Jack hares danced, not yet ready for their advances. Day came bright and clear and the jacks dispersed, each to his own place. Rik, forlorn, began the trail home to Dark Hollow. Behind him, the enticing scent and the smell of clover lay everywhere. He did not know where to go.

At last he chose a resting place at the edge of the moor.

The field was close. He would return that night and join the dancing hares. He dug himself a shallow scrape and lay flat against the earth, his breathing mothwing soft, so quiet that nothing that came near could hear him. He could see all around him, and he could see too that men worked on the field, and that their long straight gashes scored it from end to end, and bisected the grass. He had never seen such a big field before, nor had he seen such large patches of sweet clover, and for clover he would travel miles and swim rivers. He settled closer against the ground and sneezed softly, once and again.

14

A New Spring

The sun was stronger than it had been for weeks. There were dandelions growing, almost under Rik's nose, and under his forepaws was soft moss and behind him a shaggy clump of heather, the twigs dry and brittle and winter-black, but new growth coming. Beyond him miniature curled fronds of bracken forced through the black soil. The sun shone on them and stirred the trapped smells that lay in the ground. There was moss smell and grass smell and new thyme with a stinging tang when the leaves were broken, and over everything lay the spring smell of promise, of adventure, of events as yet unknown and unimaginable.

The sun faded in the west in a blaze of colour. Red reflections lay in the water of every pool and puddle, scarlet streamers fled across the black cloud, crimson shadows tinged new leaves so small that they barely showed on the trees.

Moonlight was early. Rik loped over the furrows. He was a small lonely shape, glimpsed from a passing train, and he went about his business. He was full-grown, but not yet fully developed. This he soon discovered. He met a big buck, in his fifth year, as he followed his previous day's trail to the big meadow.

The buck had seen Kee and was anxious to follow her.

Tonight he had no wish to join the dancing. He had other needs to satisfy. When Rik approached he stood erect. Rik, looking up, saw a massive animal, heavy with the weight of years, with the solidity that came with age, with the ferocity that matched his size. The buck lashed out a forepaw and at once Rik was defending himself, fighting back, desperately, for the first time in his life, parrying each blow, feeling the pain of each hard thump on his body. His own blows were puny by comparison.

He leaped sideways and the buck followed and raked with clawed hind-feet. Rik was bowled over, gasping, breathless, his side scored by sharp claws. The buck loped away, not bothering to look back, knowing himself the victor. That night Rik crept back to his form on the edge of the moor, too sore to join in the dancing.

Two nights later he was back. This time there were four does watching, one his own age. He approached her, excited, but she had no eyes for him. There were older, stronger bucks and she knew that in strength lay the protection of any babies that might be hers. Rik was too young to interest her. He was not yet grown. He had won no battles. He had no chance.

Soon there were no more does, but the remaining Jack hares had forgotten why they had gone there in the first place. Night after night they danced and fought and tumbled one another with lashing paws. It was practice for another year, for another time, and perhaps another place, when they would be the older bucks and would chase away the youngsters. It was preparation for the future, and helped to strengthen their muscles so that, when danger came calling, they could race on long legs and foil the hunter.

Yet, like everything else, the madness passed. March was succeeded by April and the hares separated, each to his own life. April fled by and May came, and blossom on the trees and growth everywhere, so that there was food in plenty. Winter was remote, a teasing memory.

Rik watched with interest as leverets were born in the fields. Several times he came upon Kee or one of the smaller does feeding her younglings, each one alone in its place, and he felt a yearning for something that he missed, but did not know what.

Meanwhile the gashes across the field grew longer and the bare earth was covered with hard concrete: the big bulldozers rattled off to new jobs, and for a brief while nothing more happened. In June, builders came, and lorries, bricks and concrete mixers, and once more Rik knew the hum and whine of machinery. He had nowhere left to go.

He returned once to Dark Hollow but the ground was sour with rubbish, the garbage dropped in the pool had killed the fish and the bright water had gone. The pool lay dark and foetid, slimed and stagnant, and nothing grew under the dying trees. There was no place for him. There were no birds. Not even the fieldmice stayed. Only the rats remained, multiplying in the burrows that had once belonged to the kingfisher. The kingfisher family died, the bright feathers were forgotten, lying muddied on the bank. The poisoned fish had killed the birds.

The year passed, with high summer brighter and hotter than it had ever been, scorching the grass, so that once more the creatures that fed on herbage knew privation. There was clover in the far corner of the airfield, and the grass was green where the builders flung their water, or where the hoses lay that were used to mix the cement. The hares hunted for the wet patches, night after night, and began to forage far afield, looking for grass that grew near water, looking for sow thistles and chicory, and finding cabbage and young lettuce. Many nursery gardeners suffered from feeding hares that year.

The days fled by to the end of the year: gale and thunder, storm, wind and snow, all repeated themselves. Rik loved thunder, he enjoyed the drumroll echo in the sky, and was mystified by the flashes that cleaved the dark. He was fully grown, heavy, and knew he was wise. He had endured the night of the Great Wind, he had watched his homeplace change until it was unrecognizable, he had travelled the hard roads and crossed the big moor, fled from gunshot and hunting dog, from running fox, hawk, owl and kestrel. He was quick to bolt from danger. He knew car, train and aeroplane. His wits were as keen as his heels were swift.

The airport grew. The runways were finished, the hangars and offices built, the high fences erected. The fences kept out dogs and foxes: they kept out people too, and soon the hares learned that the great shapes that thundered out of the dark were unable to leave the concrete runways. The hares had total sanctuary. Only the owl could find them here, only the fleeting hawk could stoop to kill. There was no place for poachers, or for chasing dogs, and the marauding foxes preferred to hunt where there was a variety of food.

By May, there were new leverets on the field, and Rik's sons and daughters were among them. He heard the does' soft call of 'oont, oont' as they went to suckle the younglings, and his paths often crossed theirs as he foraged for grass, and for the sweet clover that grew thickly in places close to the runways. He grew daring, so that sometimes, when planes came down at dusk, children, looking from the windows, saw him as he stood erect and watched, and then bounded slowly away, knowing the taxiing plane could not reach him, for it would never leave its familiar path, which was as well used as Rik's own tracks across the enormous field. The children laughed and pointed, and shouted:

'Look ! There's a hare.'

Rik loped off and hid until the plane had gone by. The thunder of its engines cut the silent air. The earth-shake as it landed vibrated the ground, and Rik lay low, a flattened hump, blending into the ground, pretending he had ceased existence, and nothing could be seen of him but a faint tremor in the grass as he breathed gently.

When silence returned, he left his form and browsed again on the clover. He was safe here for the rest of his life. He did not know that he would grow old and, twelve years later, die peacefully here, one of the many hares that had been driven away from his home and found that man had built him a special place where he could live undisturbed. He had left Dark Hollow for ever and become an airport hare, feeding fat on the long grass that was never trampled or spoiled.

At night, lights blazed along the runways and the planes fled swiftly down the airlanes coming in to land, and the weary crew, walking thankfully away to their beds, saw the brown hares watching them, grinned, and went away, little thinking of the changes these hares had seen in their lifetime.

Far away, Dark Hollow, where he had been born, lay

empty, except for the rats and the rubbish, and no birds sang there. Nothing grew, and soon even the hare that had marauded the gardens was a faint memory.

No one knew that, when the people slept, the hare that had once lived in Dark Hollow browsed in the grass at the airport, six miles away from the wood where he had been born. Nor did they know that when they flew up into the sky, leaving for their holidays, Rik and his companions lay in the long grass and watched, and cuddled down closer against the ground, and sneezed softly, warm and safe, then groomed themselves.

And in the shadowy night, when no planes landed, the only creatures that moved in the waving grass were the small brown hares.

STAY ON

Here are details of other exciting TARGET titles. If you cannot obtain these books from your local bookshop, or newsagent, write to the address below listing the titles you would like and enclosing cheque or postal order— *not* currency—including 7p per book to cover packing and postage; 2–4 books, 5p per copy; 5–8 books, 4p per copy.

TARGET BOOKS,
Universal-Tandem Publishing Co.,
14 Gloucester Road,
London SW7 4RD

TEMBA DAWN, MY CALF   30p

Alec Lea

0 426 10786 1

Rob slipped out of the farm house, crept behind the big barns, and clambered over the gate into the nursery. He peered at the heifers in the dawn light. Had Tarbo given birth to his tenth-birthday present yet? Suddenly he heard a grunt in one corner, and looked straight into Tarbo's wide eyes. As Rob watched, the calf's legs slithered out, followed by its nose and then the whole head, its eyes opening and shutting, its mouth gasping for breath . . . what a super birthday present!

THE PONY PLOT
Sara Herbert
0 426 10962 7

35P

When Lynn moves to the country, she expects life to be rather unexciting. But just days after making friends with the Barrington family, one of their ponies vanishes without trace. Lynn agrees to help in the search, but suspects that Marie and Jake, her gypsy friends from the nearby circus, are somehow involved with the mysterious disappearance. And who is Clive, the boy with the sad, haunting face. . . ? *First title in the Target Pony Mystery series.*

CREATURES OF THE BAY
Christopher Reynolds
0 426 10823 x

35P

The author's lovingly written diary which tells of the seaside life that he has discovered in the bay near to his home, and observed closely through the changing seasons of the year. Birds, shells, fishes, seaweeds, rockpool life – nothing is too minute to escape his keen eye and natural curiosity – are brought vividly to life in his beautifully illustrated book.

HAUNTED HOUSES
Bernhardt J. Hurwood
0 426 10559 1   **A Target Mystery**

30p

Who was the ghost of Powis Castle? Why has he not been seen for 200 years? What was the cause of the fatal curse on Mouse Tower? And why does Anne Boleyn ride headless with a coach and four around the grounds of Blicking Hall? Here are 25 spine-chilling tales to spirit you away . . . into HAUNTED HOUSES! *Illustrated.*

THAT MAD, BAD BADGER
Molly Burkett
0 426 10399 4

25p

A blow-by-blow true account of life with 'Nikki' the badger, who delights in whipping laces out of the shoes of unsuspecting visitors to the Burkett household, stealing goodies from the 'fridge, and lying tummyside-up in a comfortable armchair for a quiet snooze. There have been other stories about badgers, but never one like this! *Illustrated.*

DOCTOR WHO – THE THREE DOCTORS 35p
Terrance Dicks

o 426 10938 4

The most amazing WHO adventure yet, in which Doctors One, Two and Three cross time and space and come together to fight a ruthlessly dangerous enemy – OMEGA. Once a Time Lord, now exiled to a black hole in space, Omega is seeking a bitter and deadly revenge aganist the whole Universe . .

FAMOUS HISTORICAL MYSTERIES 35p
Leonard Gribble

o 426 10428 5

Ten of the most famous and intriguing mysteries in international history, many of them still unsolved today. Try and discover the truth beneath the facts and fallacies which surround, among others: Anastasia, Princess of Russia; The Dreyfus Case; the disappearance of Amelia Earhart; the *Mary Celeste*, ghost-ship; and the secret identity of the Prisoner in the Iron Mask . . . *Illustrated.*

THE NOEL STREATFEILD CHRISTMAS HOLIDAY BOOK 40p
An Anthology

o 426 10911 2

What does Christmas mean to you? Skating far away over a frozen lake, a busy excited shopping street, decorating a tree or the flowering of a Christmas rose? Join Noel Streatfeild in this lovely collection of stories from all over the world and fall head over heels into the magic of Christmas. *Illustrated.*

ABANDONED! 30p
G. D. Griffiths

o 426 10460 9

A kitten, heartlessly abandoned when 12 weeks old, gradually accepts the loss of her comfort and security, and learns to survive in the grim and savage wilds of storm-racked Dartmoor, several times cheating a cruel death before eventually finding the love and security she secretly longs for. *Illustrated*

RUNNER-UP TITLE FOR THE 1973 WHITBREAD LITERARY AWARD (CHILDREN'S BOOK DIVISION)

THE SECRET OF THE MISSING FOAL   35P
Sara Herbert

0 426 10970 8

When Ralph, Judy, Ginny, Sam and Prissy arrive at their uncle's lonely old house on the moors, they tumble straight into the thick of a wicked plot. What has caused Uncle Benedict's sudden and mysterious death? Where is his precious palomino foal? Then Prissy disappears – and doesn't come back . . . The answer must be in the nonsense rhyme the children discover in their uncle's study – but can they unravel the answer before it is too late? *Second title in the Target Pony Mystery series.*

DOCTOR WHO AND THE PLANET OF THE SPIDERS   35P
Terrance Dicks

0 426 10655 5

'It's happening, Brigadier! It's happening!' Sarah cried out. The Brigadier watched, fascinated, as the lifeless body of his old friend and companion DOCTOR WHO suddenly began to glow with an eerie golden light . . . The features were blurring, changing. 'Well bless my soul,' said the Brigadier. 'WHO will he be next?' *Read the last exciting adventure of Dr Who's 3rd Incarnation!*

DOCTOR WHO AND THE GREEN DEATH   35P
Malcolm Hulke

0 426 10647 4

The Green Death begins slowly. In a small Welsh mining village a man emerges from the disused colliery covered in a green fungus. Minutes later he is dead. UNIT, Jo Grant and DOCTOR WHO in tow, arrive on the scene to investigate, but strangely reluctant to assist their enquiries is Dr Stevens, director of the local refinery, *Panorama Chemicals*. Are they in time to destroy the mysterious power which threatens them all before the whole village, and even the world, is wiped out by a deadly swarm of green maggots? *Illustrated.*

THE ADVENTURES OF RAMA

G. Krishnamurti

35p

0 426 10364 5

Rama, a noble and kindly Indian prince, is cast into a 14-year
exile by his stepfather and is followed into the forests by his
beautiful wife, Sita, and his devoted brother, Lakshmana.
Together they encounter and destroy various demons. Eventually, Sita is kidnapped by Ravana, the ten-headed demon
king, who bears her away to Lanka. Rama promptly marches
on Lanka, accompanied by Hanuman, the beloved Monkey-
God of India, in order to rescue his beloved wife from the
cruel clutches of the fierce demon king.

DOCTOR WHO AND THE GIANT ROBOT

35p

Terrance Dicks

0 426 10858 2

'Look, Brigadier! It's growing!' screamed Sarah. The Brigadier
stared in amazement as the Robot began to grow . . . and grow
. . . and grow to the size of a giant! Slowly the metal colossus
began to stride towards the Brigadier. Its giant metal hand
reached down to grasp him . . . Can DOCTOR WHO defeat
the evil forces controlling the Robot before they execute their
plans to blackmail—or destroy—the world? *The first adventure
in DOCTOR WHO'S 4th incredible Incarnation!*

GHOSTS AND SPIRITS OF MANY LANDS

30p

Freya Littledale

0 426 10735 7

EVIL GHOSTS disappear if you read backwards . . . make
cake-mix from human blood . . . are clawed to death by
painted cats . . . STUPID SPIRITS can be trapped in a
bottle . . . cry out from the grave for lost shoes . . . FRIENDLY
GHOSTS become a path through the forest . . . make faithful
pets . . . TROUBLESOME SPIRITS shake the bed curtains
. . . bite like mosquitoes . . . talk through the mouth of a
skull . . . *Illustrated.*

THE 2nd TARGET BOOK OF FUN AND GAMES 30p

Nicola Davies

0 426 10532 X

A further book of fun and games to tease and test your wits:
jokes; riddles; tongue-twisters; mazes; experiments; funny
poems; picture-puzzles; tricks; cartoons; and never a dull
moment!

If you enjoyed this book and would like to have information
sent you about other TARGET titles, write to the address below.

You will also receive:

A FREE TARGET BADGE!

Based on the TARGET BOOKS symbol—see front cover of this
book—this attractive three-colour badge, pinned to your
blazer-lapel, or jumper, will excite the interest and comment
of all your friends!

and you will be further entitled to:

FREE ENTRY INTO THE TARGET DRAW!

All you have to do is cut off the coupon beneath, write on it
your name and address *in block capitals,* and pin it to your
letter. You will be advised of your lucky draw number.
Twice a year, in June and December, numbers will be drawn
'from the hat' and the winner will receive a complete year's
set of TARGET books.

Write to: TARGET BOOKS,
Universal-Tandem Publishing Co.,
14 Gloucester Road,
London SW7 4RD

———————————— cut here ————————————

Full name...

Address...

....

.... County.......................................

Age............................